Body and Blood

a novel of linked stories

Philip Russell

BkMk PRESS

THE UNIVERSITY OF MISSOURI–KANSAS CITY

Managing Editor
BkMk Press of UMKC
University House
5100 Rockhill Road
Kansas City, MO 64110-2499

 Financial assistance for this book has been provided by the Missouri Arts Council, a state agency.

Cover art by Anthony Russo.
Cover design by Louise Fili.

Library of Congress Cataloging-in-Publication Data

Russell, Philip, 1951–
    Body and blood / Philip Russell.
        p.   cm.
    ISBN 1–886157–15–4 (pbk.)
    I. Title.
    PS3568.U7686B6   1998
    813'.54--dc21   98–14595
                                                  CIP

This book was typeset in Times New Roman, with titles set in Poppl-Laudatio.

Printed in the United States of America on acid-free paper.

10 9 8 7 6 5 4 3 2 1

Grateful acknowledgment is made to the editors of the following magazines in which earlier versions of these stories first appeared:

The Black Water Review: "Black Water"
blueLINE: "Promises" (as "Interspace") and "Birth"
The Capilano Review: "Halloween"
CrazyQuilt: "Chimes"
Jabberwock: "Caesura"
Java Snob Review: "Alice Bourne"
Jeopardy: "Loving"
Lynx Eye: "Courtship" and "Taking Back What's Mine"
Minimus: "Transformations"
Porcupine Literary Arts Magazine: "The Ocean at Night"
SlugFest, Ltd.: "Alice Bourne" and "Black Water"
Standing Wave: "The Lemon Fair"
Sun Dog: The Southeast Review: "Let the Lies Begin"
The Wascana Review: "Two Wings of a Bird"
Westview: "Blackberries"
Wind: "Killing"
The Wolf Head Quarterly: "Chimes"
The Worcester Review: "Alice Bourne"
YoMiMoNo: "Black Water"

"The Song of Wandering Aengus," by W.B. Yeats, appearing in Chapter 6: Hollow Lands and Hilly Lands, is reprinted with the permission of Scribner, a division of Simon & Schuster, from *The Collected Works of W. B. Yeats, Volume 1: The Poems*, revised and edited by Richard J. Finneran (New York: Scribner, 1997).

To my daughter Whitney and my teacher Ellen.

CONTENTS

BODY AND BLOOD

a novel of linked stories

CHAPTER 1

Promises

Matt

I knew things had come apart when I discovered the beaver dead, a lumpy brown thing stiffening in the bright sun. He was stretched full length over the sharp branches that stuck out everywhere through his dam, and water glinted all around him. He had been shot eight times as far as I could tell, but it was hard to be sure; his fur was thick with sticky blood and he was a little pulpy. John's dog got to him before I did.

The dog was waiting for me after school; he was right there by the road when I got off the bus, thumping his tail in the gravel. They called him my dog, but he was still John's dog really, even though John gave him to me when I moved into his house last fall with ma. He was a runty animal and not very smart. I wanted to get my own dog back then.

The dog and I went up to the beaver pond together. It was mid-spring and the trees were close to full leaf; the woods smelled damp and new. I was just thinking how nice it was, how it reminded me of walks with ma. The ferns were just starting to unroll and the first trillium were in flower. Then the dog ran past me, his nose right in the dirt and the hair rising all up and down his backbone.

He didn't make a sound until he found the beaver, up at the far end of the dam. He hesitated at first—his legs stiffened and his shoulders rose, and that's when he started to bark. He was a fair-sized dog for a runt, but he had a yippy little bark. It always sounded like he was being shocked. He nudged the beaver's body some, to make sure it was really dead, I guess, and then he licked it a little, and finally he just sank his teeth into its shoulders and started to drag it off, probably to eat it.

Well, that made me mad. I yelled at the dog, and I began to chase him. When he started running I threw rocks at him, and I hit him twice. The first rock glanced off his ribs but the second was a solid hit on his shoulder. That was a good shot—I heard the dull thud of stone on muscle and bone—and I almost caught him then, but he dropped the beaver and took off, favoring his front leg but still moving pretty fast.

We had followed that beaver all spring, my ma and I, as he built his house stick by stick in the marshy part of the brook. Ma was the first one who ever saw him, out on one of her long solitary walks, and later she showed him to me. Sometimes she'd go out by herself to watch him and sometimes we'd go together. He was always at it, working away, cutting down trees, dragging branches, packing mud. When the brook went down after the snow melt he built a dam to make the water deeper around his house. I never saw an animal work so hard. He was constantly plugging leaks in the dam where the stream wanted to wash it out. The water was relentless, undermining everything and trying to take it all apart. The beaver made me think of ma somehow, trying so hard to put a home together, working like crazy, always patching things up.

I never really wanted ma to move out to John's house. I liked life the way it was—in town things were relaxed and there weren't many rules. It was always just the two of us— there was never any father. Ma was twenty-nine, but she didn't seem that old. We'd just started to do a lot of stuff together.

We moved last November, around my thirteenth birthday. The leaves were all falling, and everything was bare. Ma gave me a hunting bow, a full-sized compound model with pulleys; I'd wanted one for more than two years. She said that since we were going to live in the country I could practice with it, John could teach me how to use it, and next fall maybe he'd take me deer hunting with him. Well, he hadn't taught me anything yet.

John was forty, and he seemed as old as people get. Ma seemed older when she was with him, and he wanted me to be older, too. I don't think he ever remembered being a kid himself, and he never seemed to have much use for me, except when ma was around. There was a lot the three of us never talked about. Like why I had to stay with my grandmother when they went to Florida the week after Christmas. Or why my bedroom was going to be moved from the second floor to the first. Or really basic stuff—like how John fit in. Or how *I* did.

I'd been up to the brook a dozen times with ma to see the beaver, but I never once showed it to John. I don't know if ma ever did, either. I wondered about that as I walked back to the house to get a shovel from the tool shed. I buried the beaver on the small hill overlooking the pond and the marshy brook.

That night, when I told ma, she said, "It was that Thompson kid, Matt. I knew it." She was making spaghetti for dinner, and cooking fiddleheads, even though neither of us liked them. "He's been carrying his gun around here all spring. I knew something like this would happen." She put her long fork down and leaned against the wooden counter. "I never have trusted that kid." She rubbed her forehead and pushed her brown hair back several times, even though it wasn't out of place to begin with. "I went up there this morning to talk to his parents."

John was late again that night, and ma and I finally started dinner without him. We were almost finished eating when he came into the house. We told him about the beaver, and ma said, "You'll have to go up there."

"Susan, it's just a beaver," he said. "They cause a lot of damage." John sat down at the kitchen table. "And how do you know the Thompson kid was the one who shot it?"

Ma jumped up. "Just a beaver? How do I know who shot it? Who else would shoot it?" She went to the stove and began to bang out cold spaghetti onto a plate. I thought it might break. "He's always hanging around here with his gun. You wouldn't know. You're never here." She slammed the plate down in front of him. "I see him walking up and down the road, that dumb mean smile on his face.... Why doesn't his father make him go to school?" She left his fiddleheads on the stove.

John looked like he'd lost his balance. "Susan—"

"I don't like it, John." Ma sat down again. "I'm afraid of him. That whole family's inbred."

"I'll protect you, Ma," I said to her. I looked at John, though. "Don't worry. I'm a good shot."

John had just picked up his fork but he put it down and sat back to look at me. I stared right back until he turned to ma and said, "Up until tonight you've never mentioned the Thompson kid."

"That's just what I mean. I've complained about him before. I didn't tell you, but I went up to their trailer this morning—"

"You did?"

"—to complain to his father. He said he'd talk to his son." Ma shook her head and her long hair was pretty in motion. "Yeah, so now he's shot Matt's beaver. Great talk." She reached across the table and took John's hand. "*You'll* have to go up this time. Tonight, after dinner." She looked right into his eyes. "He's dangerous, John. He's dangerous to me and Matt."

"Susan, there's no proof it was the Thompson kid. I've never had any problems with him before."

Ma snatched her hand back. "Are you saying you won't go? You won't protect me and Matt?"

"He's scared, ma."

"Matt, shut up," ma said.

John got up from the table then without another word. He left the house with his dinner unfinished, got into his truck, and drove the quarter mile or so up the road to where the Thompsons lived. I slipped out of the house without telling ma and took a shortcut through the woods. I'd checked the place out before; it was a real dump, and creepy. There were two old trailers pushed together, and a couple of rusty cars in the yard, one upside down. A burnt-out logging truck was at the side of the driveway; weeds grew up through its bed. I crept up behind the truck. All the kids seemed to be inside the trailer—I could hear the television way in the back.

Old man Thompson met John at the door. He didn't ask him in, even though it was starting to get cold. He stood just inside the ripped screen drinking a beer, and I could see him frown as John described ma's worry about his kid.

"I know," Thompson said. "She was up this morning. Good looking woman."

"Look," said John, "we've got a boy there at home, and a dog, and your son can't be firing—"

"You ain't married to that woman, are you?"

"—and your son can't be firing his rifle around the place. It's too close to the house."

"It's just a .22," said Thompson. "Boy'll shoot where he wants, I guess."

"If he shoots around my house again you'll have to take his rifle away."

"Can't do that. Just bought it. Christmas present."

I heard John tell him about the beaver being shot. Thompson said, "Beavers ain't out of season."

I listened to John explain that it was sort of like a pet, that ma had watched it build its house this spring. Thompson didn't say anything; he just drank his beer down. Then he started to talk about raccoons. "That's fun. Find them up in the trees at night. Shoot them with lights."

John said, "Just tell your boy not to shoot around my house." Then he turned to go.

Thompson said, "Money for the skins, too." John walked back to his truck.

That night I listened to John talk to ma, their voices indistinct through the bedroom wall. I couldn't understand what they were saying. I would have gone out into the hallway and listened through their door, but John had caught me doing that the week before. The last thing I remember before I fell asleep was wishing I was bigger. I was dreaming about the marshy brook, the water flowing through the leaky dam, flowing out and away, when four gunshots woke me up.

I jumped out of bed, grabbed my bow and arrows, and ran to ma's room. I burst through the door and I shouted, "Ma, it's the Thompson kid. I know it."

Ma was already awake; she was shaking John by the shoulders and yelling right into his face. She was shaking some herself, and she was also shouting, "It's the Thompson kid."

John was finally waking up and I could tell he was trying to make sense of the noise; his mind seemed pretty slow. He knocked down the telephone and called the state police. When the dispatcher answered all he said at first was, "It's the Thompson kid."

The first trooper arrived in about ten minutes; he came in and talked with ma and John for a little while. I could tell he was stalling, waiting for his backup. He had a lot of pimples for a policeman, and he smelled like he needed a shower. He had striped pants, though, and a wide shiny belt with his pistol, handcuffs, and walkie-talkie attached, and eighteen bullets pushed down into little leather loops. When the second car arrived he went out into the dark, and ma and John were very quiet. The door burst open after a moment and the pimply trooper came back in, got John, and then went outside again.

But none of them found anything. The backup trooper said the shots we heard were probably from raccoon hunters. The pimply trooper said he'd come back in the morning, check things out in daylight, and stop up at the Thompson's trailer.

At breakfast that morning I couldn't find the dog. John told me that it was nothing to worry about, that the dog had roamed before, his dog had always roamed, but ma was pretty sure the dog had been shot, and I agreed with her. Ma insisted that John go out and look, but she wouldn't let me go with him.

John said ma was overreacting. "Susan, don't you remember?" he asked. "Three mornings ago he was missing. He came home that night."

But ma demanded, "You *have* to look." She had her hands on the hips of her tight jeans, and she looked small and solid. "You can't go to work until you find Matt's dog."

John went out to his shop where the dog normally slept at night—he'd never been able to housebreak it—and checked the tool shed and the yard. Ma stood with me in the kitchen doorway. I put my arm around her shoulders. When John returned across the grass his good shoes and the cuffs of his dress pants were soaked with dew. Ma called out to him, "Well, did you find him?" John shook his head; as he walked to the house he said everything looked normal—there was no blood anywhere and certainly no body around. "Did you look up by the brook?" ma asked. "What about the woods by the garden? Did you look in the orchard?"

"I looked everywhere, Susan," he said. "That dog is nowhere around here." He climbed the two stairs to the kitchen door and stepped between us and went into the kitchen. I heard him complaining in there. "Susan, haven't you made any coffee yet? I'm already late for work."

"You can't just go to work like nothing happened," ma said. "They'll come back. They shot the dog so he couldn't warn us."

"Susan, be reasonable. The dog is okay." John used the kitchen towel to wipe water and grass clippings from his shoes. "There's absolutely no sign the dog was shot." He tossed the towel on the counter. "And I *have* to go to work."

I said, "Let him go, ma."

John turned on me, then: "We're going to have a talk tonight, Matt, you and me. Count on it." He put on his coat. Ma wanted him to stop at the Thompson's trailer, but he said, "The state police will do that." He suggested ma go over to her mother's after I got on the bus and the police came.

But I didn't get on the school bus. I hid in the brush close to the house and watched it drive by. I had my bow and arrows, and I was planning to guard the house. I sat in a little hollow between the roots of a large maple. I could feel its deeply corrugated bark dig into my back and I was swatting black flies and thinking about the beaver when I heard several .22 caliber rifle shots.

I looked out through the leaves of the low scrub and saw the Thompson kid walk down the road, his rifle in his big hand. I crouched down in the bushes, but the kid paused near me anyhow; he looked into the woods all around me, his mean mouth smiling. I held my breath then; I could hear the insects and the slight breeze. A fly landed right on my face but I stayed absolutely still. The Thompson kid raised the rifle to his shoulder and slowly swept the woods. At one point I could see straight down the barrel; I could see his watery eye centered over the small black bore, just behind the sight. Then the barrel moved on, and the Thompson kid finally lowered the rifle at the end of its arc. He started down the road again, heading toward ma in John's house, lazily swinging his rifle from side to side. I could hear him laugh softly; it was a dumb laugh.

I nocked an arrow onto my bowstring before he moved out of range and I drew the thick string all the way back. It was hard for me—the bow has a fifty-pound pull. I sighted down the arrow shaft, over the fluted metal tip to the center of the Thompson kid's back, and then I released the string.

But the arrow just grazed his shoulder; it didn't even knock him down. The kid screamed anyway, though, then whirled around and saw me. He raised his rifle and fired twice, but his aim was off. I ran into the woods.

Behind me I could hear everything coming together. I heard ma shouting, and then I heard John's dog barking, those yippy little barks. I heard a few more rifle shots, and bullets ripping up the leaves overhead. I heard the sound of a police siren and I just kept running.

Let them clean up their own mess. I'd done the best I could, and I knew this: I would build things solid when I grew up; I'd never just patch them together. And I would find myself some better weapons somewhere, and I'd learn how to use them. Next time, I'd know exactly what I was aiming at. And next time, I wouldn't miss.

CHAPTER 2

Alice Bourne

Alice

I've heard them whisper; I've seen them watching; I
know what people say. *Drunk. Those Bournes were all
drunks.* Doomed is more like it, I think. Although maybe
there's no real difference.

Louis Bourne. How could you just ride into the river
in the middle of a snowstorm, no matter *how* drunk you were?
Breaking through the ice in the quiet night, your car slipping
away, sinking beneath you, carrying you down to the river
bottom, the snowfall all soft and white for a moment in the
headlights, then just the water, the coldness, the black ice
silently resealing itself overhead? By sunrise, no sign.

What was it like? That alcoholic shroud, that fuzzy
cocoon, the warmth of the car heater. Then icy water displac-
ing everything, that relentless sheet curling up under the
doorsill. The river pressing the doors shut. Did you scream?
Could it matter?

Louis Bourne. Did you even *see* the ferry slip? Did
you think the ferry might still be there, that it was somehow
still summer? Last July with your eyes and then that night with
your hands all over me? Uncle Louis.

Why wasn't the chain up, anyhow?

Maybe you got the time right but the place wrong.
Perhaps you thought the river was some wind-swept field, snow
drifting over the icy road. Who knows? Maybe you thought
the ice would hold you.

Or maybe you knew it wouldn't. Perhaps you knew
what you were doing all along. Although it's possible you
weren't even the one driving. That's what I wonder about
mostly these days. Who killed the other?

Because it's hard to tell. The car wasn't found until the following spring, after the ice went out, grinding like a glacier. The current had rolled that old Pontiac downstream like some huge hollow boulder, scraping and bumping it along the river bottom, bodies floating and turning inside. My mother and Louis Bourne.

I came home for the memorial service. And after exams I returned for good. It's funny how things work out. Ever since I was a kid I couldn't wait to escape; I promised myself I'd *never* come back. I'd leave them behind forever, the drunk ones. My mother with her hard-bitten eyes. We never had one single thing in common; I don't even *look* like her—I've got Bourne eyes.

I was so sure I'd never return. But things conspire.

Bourne Mountain, Bourne Hollow, Bourne Pond—everywhere the land is named for us. My ancestors cut down an entire forest here; their farms once spread from the head of the hollow to the far side of the river. But that time is long past. Most of the Bournes disappeared a century ago, and those fields and pastures have all grown up to woods again. Nothing remains now but an occasional lilac or apple in the middle of second growth forest, some piles of fieldstone, an old bull maple. There are places up in the hollow where the road can't even be picked out anymore.

As a child I followed their rock walls snaking through the woods; I tracked down every cellar hole where any Bourne ever lived. I searched out each of their graveyards—family plots forgotten on the mountain side—scraped the moss from broken stones, traced out names and dates with my fingertips.

We were the last ones, the last of the Bournes, living in this dented blue trailer on the side of Bourne Mountain. Before my father disappeared he logged these woods for miles around—hiring out to absentee owners. He cut pulp mostly, sometimes cordwood—there's no good timber anymore. But he loved these woods, I think; he always considered the

mountain his birthright somehow. But it wasn't, of course.
Just this trailer. This trailer and ten acres, that's all that's left.
And me. Alice Bourne.

I've never been able to believe my father would just up
and quit, although that's what I've been told ever since I was
young. He would have left me some kind of word, I think,
some kind of sign. The fact is, sometimes I can still feel him
around. When I wander up through the hollow with my dog,
my father's presence is strong. I think he loved this land so
much he can't let go of it. That's not as nice as it might sound.

At night, when the moon is full, I walk the old track
along the brook that comes off the headwall of the mountain. I
think of the farms that used to be here, the women who have
been here before me, who have been me already in some way,
as if part of me is already dead, like my family. I look at old
cemetery markers, marble and slate, the unlettered fieldstone.
The women all young, and all those children. Cemeteries full
of women and children and I understand how my family came
to leave this place.

What I cannot understand is why I came back. Somehow I could have stayed at school. I could have taken a year
off, worked, saved, applied for a bigger scholarship. My
landlord found out about my dogs, but I could have found
another place to live. There was no good reason to return.

I think the land called me back. The bones buried
here. Women and children and maybe my father. Bones of
houses and barns. This is where I came from, after all. I was
rootless in the city. The air smelled like concrete and asphalt
and no history of any kind. Cracks in the sidewalks, fissures in
foundations. Who would put down roots in a place like that?
So I returned to my side of the mountain. I moved back into
the trailer and I started to work in the village library. My dogs
are my family now, and my protection. I am the last of my line;
I can feel it. The name Bourne will die with me.

Since I've returned I've been having these dreams. I see my father as a young man, gone off alone hunting deer on the shoulder of the mountain. It's a cold November morning but there's no snow and the deer are hard to track. My father is working his way up the north slope of the mountain; I can see his plaid coat dull red among the silvery maples. In my dream I see movement in the thick scrub below him; brush moves, then is still. I watch the scrub for a long time, then I see sunlight glint off gun metal.

I've been sleeping less and less well. My dreams are becoming more intense. Sometimes I wake in the middle of the night, sheets soaked with sweat. Sometimes I awaken to the sound of my own voice. And sometimes, in the dead of the night, I wake up and reach for one of their bottles.

I keep finding their bottles. Unopened, half-full, almost empty. Bottles stashed all over the trailer and the yard outside. I find them in the woodpile, in the little shed behind the dented blue trailer, where Louis kept his tools. I find them in the backs of closets, in the dark corners of cupboards, under the bed, behind the bureau. At night I find them in my sleep, waking from dreams I cannot remember. I twist off the stamped metal caps; I drink the dark liquid within.

In the morning I wake hungover and dully hungry for food and sex, but mostly I think about drinking—whether I will start, when I will start, where the bottle is.

Now it's late fall, the maples have flamed and gone out, like the oaks and birches—only the beech leaves hang on, rattling skeletal in the cold wind. What is underneath all of this? Loneliness? Rage? I reach for the bottle. I put it away. I know I'll never survive a winter alone here.

Day and night I keep walking to those isolated grave-yards. The early October moon is called the harvest moon, although around here if crops aren't gathered by October it's too late. The distance between the trailer and the cemeteries grows increasingly short. There is frost on the grave markers. The distance between the headstones and the footstones is incredibly short. Early childhood the final measure of stature. What could that life have been like, burying all those babies?

When I return to the trailer it feels as if someone's been there in my absence. The place is full of flawed passion, anger and hatred. The dogs sense it, too. I send them in ahead of me, and they enter with their heads down, growling soft and low, a constant background vibration. This trailer is small, and the dogs cover it in seconds. There is no place to hide here. The trailer is empty. But they don't relax, and I don't either.

My dreams have gotten increasingly physical. Before, I used to wake in the night with the bedclothes just twisted up and knotted. Now sometimes there's blood on the sheets, and scratches and bruises all over my body and face. Louis and my mother used to fight all the time, drunk or sober, morning or night. My mother's eyes were black so often that when I was little I thought that was her normal face. *Those Bournes are drunks.* In my dreams I don't know whose face is being hit.

There are old dreams and new dreams. Sometimes I wake, or think I wake, to a face leaning over my bed, a hand coming out of the smell of whiskey to stroke my body. Whose face? My uncle's? My father's? All I can see are those Bourne eyes, leaning over me.

The lock on my door has always been broken. When I was fifteen I got Lancelot from a neighbor who raised Kuvaszok. I always hung around their kennel after school, helping out with feeding and cleaning, taking a shift watching the bitches when they whelped. Lancelot was from a litter they couldn't sell; the puppies all looked like they'd develop hip dysplasia. And every one did, except for Lancelot. I even began to show him. But mostly he was my closest friend, and above all he slept on the foot of my bed every night, from the day I brought him home. Now I have two more dogs, and all three sleep on my bed.

Toward the end of October things become intolerable. In last night's dream the car is sinking. Louis is reaching out for me, inviting me in, his hair floating around his face. His

17

face over my bed. Lancelot growling low in his throat. In my dreams my mother is offering me a bottle, holding it up like a chalice, amber liquid glinting within. She isn't really smiling. Her mouth is hanging open, several teeth are missing, her head lolls from side to side. In my dream I see snowflakes settle on black water. Fine lacy work of ice crystals spread out like fingers across the violated opening, reaching out from the edges toward each other. In my dream I am below the surface, the icy tendrils reach across above me sealing the space. I see snowflakes come down and melt on the surface of the black water then I see them land on the surface of the new forming ice and they are not melting, they stick, they add to one another. They form a white blanket, soft, a cocoon, and the Pontiac is a chrysalis and I am in it with Louis reaching his hand toward me and my mother pushing the bottle toward me and I wait for the metamorphosis.

In the morning I wake on the floor, the sheets twisted around me, struggling to get free. That morning I collect all the bottles I can find—empty, full, half-empty—and I take them down to the ferry crossing. The ferry has closed for the season—it's almost Halloween. The leaves are down, the chain is up, the tourists are gone. I empty dark liquid onto the river's surface. The alcohol mixes with the water, everything drowns together, these spirits and their spirits and it should be moon-light, the hunter's moon. I throw the empty bottles out toward the middle of the river as far as I can. They float for a long time before sinking, glinting in the light like ice.

I consider burning the trailer down, setting the woods on fire, burning down the whole mountain, ending everything once and for all. But I don't do any of these things.

Still I know I can't stay here anymore. In my dreams the Pontiac rolls over and over, grinding along the river bottom. I've been waking with black eyes and bruised skin, struggling on the floor, Lancelot growling low in his throat, his hackles raised.

18

This is not working. Anyone can see that. I'm twenty-one. I'm Alice Bourne. I've been seeing their eyes in the dark. I should have never come back.

CHAPTER 3

Halloween

Matt

The loneliness was there first, the void waiting to be filled. Before I even knew Alice's name I was watching for her. But I never saw anything out the front window that night—only the black street glistening empty under those old-fashioned lamps, pools of dim light separated by darkness. I stood waiting, empty myself, spirit thin as rain-streaked glass, brittle and transparent. By shifting my focus slightly I could see my image in that lucent space between rain and misting breath. My face looked thin and drawn, pale—eyes larger than usual, blacker. Brown hair thick and chaotic, the day's beard heavy enough so I seemed unshaven. My face looked haunted. Hunted. An image captured under glass, like that early picture of Leslie on the wall behind me.

Primitive people still believe photography captures the soul. A confusion between image and spirit. Leslie captured *my* spirit, that's clear enough. Somewhere in Boston she still had it. All *I* had was this glossy piece of eight by ten print paper with some chemicals on it—one of my images of who I thought she might really be. I don't know why I carried that picture around: my head was full of images of Leslie, all the time, wherever I went. We'd divorced the summer before, but there's no finality to anything. Things just go on and on. Damage extends across decades, maybe lifetimes—I don't know.

The glass in the front window was older than lifetimes, small panes full of wavy ripples and occasional long ovoid bubbles. Air encased for generations—breaths of people dead now for centuries, their smells, the sounds of their voices.

Each pane was thicker at the bottom than the top, gravity over the years inexorable, making solids fluid, thinning and drawing out even molecular bonds.

I hardly recognized my face there between the layers of water and glass, trapped between surfaces, caught in that interspace. I looked like a spirit myself. A holiday spirit, for the Celtic new year, prophecies and portents and the walking dead. I'd researched it all at the newspaper: Saman calling forth evil hosts, Druids burning enormous fires to protect the people. It was a desperate time—you could smell it. Any damned soul that felt like it could wander around at will, that was the most incredible part. The other stuff was just so much junk—Pomona and the Romans and their fruit, the Christians with all their saints. It was the lord of the dead I'd been thinking about. Spirits revisiting earthly homes. Beasts. I built a fire like the rest.

I made the light that attracted her, and she came into it, the single worst thing that would ever happen to me.

I never saw anyone come up to the back porch, either; I jumped at the sound of the knock. When I opened the kitchen door it seemed Alice had just materialized there, formed out of nothing, black eye and all. Her eye wasn't magical, I'll be the first to admit. It was singularly ugly—purple turning to green and yellow, the skin all cheesy and dead-looking in the bare overhead light. It was a revolting black eye. I thought it was a joke initially, a Halloween disguise, and I stood with my hand on the door frame, trying to smile. It was hard to look casual, though; the wood was old and splintery and you couldn't comfortably lean on it.

Except for her eye she had a very elegant face—high cheekbones and a fine distinct jaw. "Guinevere did that," she said, speaking first. I nodded slowly. "My bitch," she explained, stroking her temple gently with long fingers.

She didn't wear any makeup. Generally I preferred women without makeup, but with an eye like that it was different. She looked straight at me with it. "I was just bending

down to feed her, and our heads collided. Hers was harder." I
had no idea what she was talking about. When she smiled her
lips tightened, stretching back over the narrow arch of her
teeth. That was nicer than her eye; she had a magnificent
smile. She lowered her hand and held it out to me. "I'm Alice.
I called about the apartment."

I nodded my head again. "Right." I'd forgotten about
the rental ad. "Matt," I said, and I took her hand, of course, but
I didn't believe her one bit. I was learning about this town, and
I was pretty sure some boyfriend had ruined her eye. Now here
she was turning up at my door. Great. If I rented to her there'd
be fights on the porch, me in the middle, probably blood
splattered around, maybe body parts, anything. No doubt my
editor would expect me to cover it.

I'd been advertising for a month to sublet part of this
house I couldn't afford. So far only three people had come to
look at the rooms: a thin scruffy kid clearly running away from
something; an old man without any teeth who showed up
drunk; and a pretty young woman named Jackie who couldn't
manage the security deposit and wondered if she could spread
the rent out over time. I had to say no to Jackie—I was running
out of money myself—but I've wondered since how things
might have turned out differently. Life is all so confused with
small choices, millions of them, and most of them don't mean a
damn thing, really—you could almost leave them to chance.
But always there are one or two that go on to change everything—and there's no way to tell those apart from the rest.

I lowered my gaze, not wanting to marvel at Alice's
eye too much. She wasn't wearing a jacket, although it had
been raining on and off all night—just an old reddish vest,
goose down, thoroughly faded. She wore it unsnapped over a
blue chamois shirt, tails loose and partly unbuttoned. She
didn't look cold, though—only hurriedly dressed. I stepped
back and held the door open.

She didn't act like a person who'd just gotten beaten
up, either. Alice came inside bouncing, swinging blond hair

and tight white pants. I couldn't help staring. The danger of loneliness is this: it puts you at risk.

"Can I keep dogs here?" she asked.

"I guess so." I looked at her face once more. "I like dogs all right. I had one when I was a kid." I closed the door behind her. "It was my stepfather's dog, actually."

"Great. This is the eighth place I've looked at. Landlords usually hate dogs." She stepped into the kitchen and took off her vest.

"I'm not really the landlord." I put my hand out for her vest, and hung it on the back of a kitchen chair. "I'm just subletting the place. Part of the place. Come on, I'll show you around." I was renting out the back ell, two rooms and a bathroom. Alice was walking down the hallway as if she already knew the house. "How come they hate dogs?" I asked.

"It's not just dogs; they hate kids, too." I looked at her closely. "No kids." She grinned again. "Not yet. Three dogs, though." I nodded. "Big ones."

"I should ask my landlord."

The first room was hard and glassy, with windows facing each other across a quarter-sawn oak floor. My books were still there on temporary shelves along one wall. Alice stopped to look over the titles, mostly hunting and homesteading. A lot of field guides. "I'll move those out," I said.

"Don't you read fiction?"

I frowned slightly. "You don't need to make up stories."

"Really?" She laughed, running her fingertip slowly down the row of spines. "I could change your mind about that." She pulled out a volume on bow hunting and shook her head. "I know lots of stories." Riffling through the pages, she sighed, then snapped the book shut and shelved it. "More than you've ever seen between *these* covers." She looked at me curiously. I wished she didn't have that black eye. "I'll bring you a couple of novels," she said, "and some poetry. I work in the library sometimes. Let's see the other room."

She turned on her heel and walked toward the door on the far wall. The swing of her hips was arresting. I said, "You don't look like a librarian."

"It's my eye," she answered, without bothering to look back.

The end room was smaller, with windows on three of the walls. Outside the rain had increased; you could hear it pound against the clapboards, and the glass on the northern wall was running with water. I hadn't turned on the radiators in the ell, and the room felt stark and cold. Alice shivered, and turned away after a brief glance. "It feels like a grave back here."

"I should show you these rooms in the daylight."

"And with the heat on."

I followed her back through the dining room, where she ran her fingers over the dark table of soft five-quarter pine. I thought I heard her murmur, "Leslie," as she went by, but that was impossible; it must have been "lovely."

We moved toward the fire in the living room. "These rooms we'd share, like the kitchen." My fire burned loudly, snapping on the hearth—the room smelled faintly of wood smoke. "What do you think?"

"This fire is nice. I like fires a lot." She turned slowly in front of it. "Fires are the heart of a place." She took off her chamois shirt; underneath she wore a tight knit jersey. She had wonderful breasts. When I looked back at her face I saw she was watching me, her smile amused and a little bit challenging. I bent down and poked up the fire, making it pop and spit sparks. When I turned around she'd crossed the room to the photograph on the far wall. "A pretty lady," she said, without looking at me. She leaned closer to the picture. "And pretty young."

The problem with loneliness is this: it gives everybody an opening. "Yeah. That was from Boston. When I was still a kid."

Alice came back and examined me for a moment. "You look like her a little, especially around the eyes." She turned and extended her hands toward the fire, palms open. "Pretty young," she repeated. Her hair was glowing in the firelight. It made her look like she had a halo, or at least an aura. "You're not related."

"Not anymore."

"You didn't grow up in Boston."

I looked at her back for a long moment before answering. She had a funny way of asking questions. "I grew up in Vermont. North of here. Boston's where I went to school."

"Do you like being back?"

"It's hard to meet people."

She glanced at me over her shoulder with her good eye. "That's always hard."

I shook my head. I was trying to start over, but I didn't know how to explain that to her. She stood in front of the fire and stretched languidly, hands clasped behind her head. I enjoyed watching her muscles flex, the long curve of her body arching like a bow, the fire backlighting her hair.

"Were *you* raised around here?" I asked.

"My family's always lived over the mountains," she said after a moment, without turning around.

"Do *you* like it?"

"It's okay. It's where I grew up." She shifted her weight to one leg, reaching over objects on my mantelpiece, keys and change, my jackknife, my grandfather's old pocket watch. Beyond my compass and topographic maps were a small rabbit skull I'd found and bleached, some crinoid fossils from Buttons Bay, a single dried rose and a dull yellow wedding band. "What's this?" she asked, turning toward me and holding out a small leather case.

Leslie had given me that, back when we were planning our return to Vermont together. "An Abney level. Sort of a pocket transit. I've been thinking of buying some land." I didn't remember whose idea that was anymore, hers or mine;

dreams go back and forth through time, merging together, transforming.

Alice smiled broadly. "That's a coincidence." She really did have a wonderful smile. "I've been doing that, too." She pulled the instrument out of the soft leather pouch. "How does it work?"

"You sight through the eyepiece at your target, then set the level on top. You read the degree of slope on that curved scale. It gives you the lay of the land."

"The lay of the land. Hmm." She nodded her head slowly. "I've been walking land for the past year." She sighted on the ceiling light. "I want to build a kennel."

"Why?" I asked. I'd always thought of kennels as dog jails, full of little barred doors, rows of cinder block cells, fences around fences.

"Why not? I'm tired of having people hassle me about my dogs. Plus I could make money from boarding, and do some training." She adjusted the level. "Mostly I want to do some serious breeding."

"Serious breeding," I repeated without thinking.

She looked at me through the eyepiece. "Dogs. My dogs are registered kuvaszok. Guard dogs for sheep."

"Never heard of them." I smiled. "Sorry."

"I have two bitches and a dog, all early bloodlines." She lowered the level. "I've been saving for three years now." She frowned. "It's hard."

I nodded. "It's impossible."

Thin maple branches scraped the living room window. A wind was behind the rain now, taking the last leaves down. I put more wood on the fire. Alice sat on the floor in front of the fireplace, her back against the couch, and I sat close to her. I could smell her body—musty, earthy, like leaf mold. "I love fires," she said again. "They make a house alive. Like a brook on a piece of land." She leaned toward me a little. I glanced at her long white legs, my hands restless in my lap. "It's nice to be here, Matt."

She was cut off abruptly by loud banging from the kitchen door; I had to get up to answer it. Alice went to use the bathroom. There were two older kids on the porch, wanting candy, not in costume but soaking wet. I gave them most of the candy I had; they were the only children to come all night. But no sooner had they run off than two more figures came up the walk—a misshapen yellow form bent awkwardly over a shorter, darker one, shielding it from the rain. In the circle of porch light I saw they were actually three people: a tough-looking little kid and his young mother, who carried a child of three or four on her hip. Those two were wrapped in a dull yellow raincoat; I guessed her husband's.

I let them all right inside; it was insane to carry a little child around in that cold rain. The woman was pretty, with short black hair, squarely cut. She unbuckled her raincoat and put her daughter down on the floor. Under the raincoat her body looked lithe and muscular, but I must have admired it too openly or too long, because when I glanced away I saw Alice standing in the hall doorway, studying me critically. Her frown left me uneasy, feeling guilty, remembering my one infidelity with Leslie, that time beyond reason. Sometimes I think we're as mindless as molecules, our lives directed by hormones. Insensate machines, lubricated with adrenaline, estrogen, testosterone. And not very well lubricated, either—always there's friction, endless grinding, pieces fracturing from heat and stress.

Alice knelt beside the little girl, who pointed at her eye and giggled. She was dressed in gauzy white, with a halo smashed down around her head, her hair all in her eyes. Alice brushed it out of her face, smiling. "This is the last place," the woman said, turning to her son with a reproachful look.

The boy wasn't listening, though; he was staring at me, and suddenly he shouted, "I know you! The newspaper man!" I looked him over carefully, but I didn't know him. He must have been on one of the grammar school tours I'd conducted since early September. Hundreds of children blurred together,

28

the faceless masses. My editor thought it was good public relations. This kid looked like a little gangster—he didn't need any costume.

I smiled at the woman, reached down and tousled the boy's wet head. "You should wear a hat," I told him. He frowned at me, snarling, twisted his head and snapped at my fingers with his teeth. I pulled my hand away fast. "Little shit," I thought, but I don't think I said anything out loud. Alice looked up at me, though.

After they left Alice asked, "Do you always want to sleep with every woman you meet?"

I didn't know what to answer to that one. The thing is, the woman reminded me of Leslie. After a moment I said, "Would you like some cider?"

"Have you got any wine?"

I brought a bottle into the living room. Alice followed, turning out the ceiling lights on her way. Joining me in front of the hearth, she picked up the Abney level again. "So you're not a surveyor," she said.

"Nope. I came here to work for the newspaper. I'm a reporter. Learning to be a reporter." I handed her a glass of wine.

"That sounds pretty interesting."

"Actually it's pretty boring. Except for the deadlines. The deadlines drive everyone crazy. There's a lot of stress. And you make some enemies. The paper's always looking for new people." In fact I was ready to quit, myself. The job wasn't what it was made out to be; being part of the salaried staff simply meant I didn't get paid for overtime. All autumn I'd done nothing but sit in front of my word processor until late every night, churning out copy. One night a week was all I had off, and by then I was usually so tired of people I'd hole up in my house, glad of the quiet space and the empty rooms.

"I always thought it would be exciting to be a reporter."

"I did, too." We touched glasses. "But it's not a very good job." Still, it was better than carpentry; I'd never do that again.

Once more there was knocking at the kitchen door, and I answered it frowning. Two ravaged people stood there this time, dark figures dripping water and swaying a little. The man wore a canvas hunting coat spotted with dried blood, and a gray slouch hat pulled down so low I couldn't see his face, just lank hair and beard. A woman skulked behind him, standing as far back from him as she could get and still remain sheltered by the roof. She was drenched to the skin, her skin pale and cadaverous, and her face was blotched or bruised—I couldn't tell which. When she opened her mouth several teeth were missing, and her eyes glinted like ice in the yellow porch light.

I thought she was hissing—*asshole, you asshole*—but it was hard to be sure with the rain streaming off the roof behind her. I stepped forward, but so did the dark man— lunging at me suddenly with both hands outstretched. Yet there was no weight to him; nothing at all really except wetness, coldness. I threw him off easily, pivoting to the side. "Get out of here," I said. "I'll call the trooper." And although I was braced and ready to fight him, I didn't need to—he stepped back, crouching down; he never said a word.

The hissing continued behind me, however—*asshole, you'll be so sorry you asshole*—and louder than before. But when I looked over my shoulder the porch was deserted. And when I turned back to the man in the canvas coat, he was gone too. I stepped off the porch into the dooryard.

The runoff from the eaves instantly drenched me; the rain was changing to sleet and the icy shock almost knocked me down. The yard was empty as far as I could see, and there was no sound anymore except the storm. I climbed back onto the porch and stood looking and listening for several minutes, then I went inside, closed the door and locked it.

In the living room Alice had turned off the rest of the lamps; only firelight illuminated the space. "You're soaked," she said. "What happened?"

"I'm not sure," I answered, pushing wet hair back from my face. "It's all right now, though." But my skin felt frozen. "I need to get a dry shirt and towel."

"Who was at the door?"

"A couple of hill people. Not kids. A prank, I guess." I started toward the bathroom. "Maybe connected to the newspaper."

When I returned Alice had put some music on the stereo, with the volume down low—*Appalachian Spring*, the only classical music I ever liked. It was Leslie's music, and I was positive I'd left it in Boston. "That okay?" she asked.

"I guess," I said. The music was as unsettling as everything else. "Sure," I nodded, and sat down next to her, a little closer than before, wanting most of all just to pause for a moment.

"I'd like to live here, Matt." She touched my glass a second time.

"I'd like that, too." We both drank.

We choose such ignorance sometimes.

We sat without talking for a while, sipping wine. The music filled the room like Leslie's spirit. At one point Alice moved closer to me, sliding a tiny bit across the floor so our bodies touched. She hummed something I couldn't understand; I asked her what it was. "That melody that keeps repeating is an old Quaker hymn," she explained. "'*Tis a Gift*." She sang the whole thing through, softly layering her words over the violins' melody. I leaned back against the couch and closed my eyes. I could smell Leslie's scent in the room—beautiful danger, inviting and repelling, sharp and sexual. Alice didn't speak after she finished, and the music on the tape continued quietly. At one point there was more knocking on the kitchen door. "Don't answer it," she said, and I was happy not to. The fire was warm on my face. I took a sip of wine and put my arm around her shoulders—it seemed the only thing to do.

But the knocking continued, loud and persistent, and finally I couldn't ignore it. Yet when I opened the door the porch was deserted. I walked the length of the rain-swept deck, searching the night. It was all just empty darkness, vacant coldness wetly stretching away. I turned and went back inside.

Alice was standing in front of the fire; she asked me who was there. I said, "No one. A joke. Kids." I put my hands on her shoulders, but her shoulders were cold. Her whole body was cold—I could feel the chill emanate through her clothes. I looked at her face and her black eye was just staring straight ahead. I got up to put more wood on the fire, although the room was already uncomfortably warm. Alice moved closer to the hearth. I stepped to her other side, so I wouldn't have to look at her eye.

"I should go," she said.

"Not yet."

She smiled. I reached out to her. She shook her head. "I'll stop by tomorrow," she said; then she was gone.

From the porch I watched her car's lights dim and then disappear into the wet darkness. But I didn't stand there staring after they winked out—it was too cold and raw. Winter was coming fast; you could smell that, too. I went inside to the fire and sat on the floor with my back against the couch, the heat and light full in my face. I slid my hand into my pocket, my fingertips touching the slip of paper with her phone number. I closed my eyes. The danger of loneliness is this: you get used to it. And getting used to it isn't as hard as it should be. After a while it doesn't even seem wrong. That's the scary part.

I got up once to get the wine bottle and refilled my glass. I sat there for a long time, watching the fire burn down to embers, sipping the wine, filled with the bitter red glowing of it. I tried to recall the sound of Alice's voice, but couldn't, so I replayed the music she'd chosen, listening carefully, trying to hear the exact sound of her song. But I only remembered two lines, *'Tis a gift to be simple, 'tis a gift to be free.* And I never heard her voice at all.

I put more wood on the coals, and tried to recall her face, but couldn't do that either. Not with any precision. The sweep of blond hair across her forehead was clear enough, but

where it fell on her head and shoulders the detail blurred. I
could picture her blue eyes distinctly—the large pupils and
striated iris—but the face around them was hazy and dull.
Even her injured skin was hard to see definitely. There was a
clear image of very fine, downy blond facial hair, the fire
backlighting her profile. I could see her wide grin, her com-
pressed lips, but the delicate angularity of her cheekbones and
jaw went in and out of focus, never stopping at a place that was
real. I couldn't recall the shape of her body, and the harder I
tried, the more indistinct everything became.

There was a noise at the door, but it was clear through
the side window it wasn't Alice, and I closed my eyes again
and sipped some more wine, trying to solidify things, wishing it
were already tomorrow. I felt as if I were standing on the edge
of my life, shifting centers, putting into motion a thing without
limits.

Sitting still became impossible. I got up and wandered
through the empty house, looking for any tangible evidence of
her visit, wanting to touch things she'd touched, trying to make
things concrete. I went back to the ell, flipped on the light in
the first room and pulled out my volume on bow hunting,
riffling through the pages as she had. I went further back, but
there was nothing in the last room except black rain-streaked
glass. I tried to feel it as Alice's room, but it felt like the
outside, smelled cold and raw, and I left quickly, thinking of
graves.

In the bathroom there was a hairbrush like Leslie's,
and under the chair in the kitchen I found a large dog biscuit
that must have fallen out of Alice's down vest. Near it were
two tiny white feathers, no bigger than my thumbnail. I picked
them up and went back to the living room. Her wine glass
stood on the floor next to the hearth. I looked on the mantle for
the Abney level, but it wasn't there—a volume of Yeats lay in
its place instead. I read the poem the book opened to, about a
man who once glimpsed a magical girl, then spent the rest of
his life searching for her. The lines made me sad and I closed

the book, put it back on the scarred wood and set the feathers on the worn green cover. I sat against the couch again, the fire hypnotic and glowing. The warmth and the wine made me sleepy, and I dozed off to dream about a beast with black eyes. The danger of loneliness is this: you tend to adopt it. It's so small at first, sniffing around, that you feel sorry for it. You talk to it and pet it and after a while start to feed it. Eventually you give it a name. With each day it grows larger. Soon it needs always to be fed. It sits on your hearth each night, waiting for your return. You can never feed it enough. Finally you understand that it's *you* the beast wants to consume.

I woke up convinced I heard breathing. The fire had almost gone out and the room was dark. I shook my head in disgust. I'd been there before; it was just a trap. Leslie never kept the beast away; somehow she *became* the beast. Too much loneliness and too much testosterone, a hopeless combination.

I piled more wood on the fire. The dry pine caught quickly; soon flames chased each other up the chimney. I watched the flames and listened to the quiet of the house settle around me, and for just a moment everything felt held at bay, almost peaceful. I felt full of sudden resolve—I'd call Alice and just tell her my landlord wouldn't accept dogs, period. I'd concentrate on remembering her black eye.

I looked at my watch. It still wasn't that late, so I picked up the telephone. Alice answered on the first ring. She said "Matt" before I could speak. She sounded just like Leslie. I could hear her breathing across the telephone lines. I closed my eyes. The wine made me feel dizzy. Spirits filled the room, souls wandering around at will. In the quietness of my house I could hear breathing. "Come on over," she said.

And all I could feel then was an aching in my heart. Or perhaps it was between my legs. I don't know. I feel like that machine sometimes, a body, an animal thing, a beast myself, intent on its own destruction. Alice was silent a long time, waiting for me to speak. Finally I said, "How do I get there?"

CHAPTER 4

Courtship
Matt

Maybe there is no beginning or end to things, and no escape—just longing, repetition and doom. I'm not certain anymore. I *did* answer her call, even though it was midnight, the storm still ascendant—rain changing to hail and finally to snow by the time I reached the darkness of Bourne Mountain and Alice. Night rent with lightning, ripped trees exploding—still, I was pleased as a man could be when I turned off the highway, engaged four-wheel-drive, and began the grinding climb up into the hollow. Thunder smashed down the mountain in breaking waves, heavy with sleet, and her road was gullied like a river, the ground frozen almost solid, thick with water rolling unchecked off hillsides. The lightning was brilliant and fast; my eyes couldn't adjust to the strobing, the pulsing interruptions of blackness, and I drove into memory—dark trees and gutted road, the black forest overall. Lightning struck close by and a tree crashed down behind me. Halfway up the hollow broken trunks and splintered limbs completely blocked my way; I had to shut off the truck and proceed on foot. With each strike, a vivid flash—for an instant I could move forward into afterimage, then darkness halted me once more. I continued like that, dazzled, bursts of brilliant light punctuating utter blackness, all the rest of the way to Alice's trailer.

Which I almost passed in the night, because the storm had taken the power down, but her dogs began to bark at me, and forked branches of lightning lit up the sky; for a second her blue trailer stretched out long and low, then thunder crashed down darkness again. The door banged open and Alice stood on the threshold with a flashlight, dogs swirling around her feet. I pressed inside, wrestling with the door and the shrieking wind, a roaring primordial thing straining to tear the flimsy aluminum out of my hands, challenging my entry, my right to be there, my very existence. Finally I was able to secure the door, and the sudden silence within. Alice stood in silhouette, backlit by candles. "Welcome," she said quietly, and kissed me on my lips.

And when I think of Alice now, what I remember most is her welcome that night. The fall of her nightgown from her breasts to her ankles, nipples hard against white gauzy fabric, the shadow of her sex beneath. Maybe there is only one first time for anything, never a second—maybe we *are* condemned to just repeat our past. I can't say. I'd like to think there was some decision, some moment of volition, at least an instant of free will. I'd like to think I chose to go to Alice Bourne that night.

I took off my coat and hung it beside her door. Alice drew close and our bodies touched; my fingertips slowly traced her back from her fine shoulder blades to the soft curve of her buttocks. The storm beat against the roof and the thin metal walls; the wind rocked the whole trailer on its cinderblock piers, and the floor shuddered under our feet. The dogs were quiet now, black tongues and lips, smiling. Alice took a candle and led me to her bedroom. Her dogs followed, watching, dark eyes and mouthfuls of white teeth. Alice sat on the bed and extended both hands. "I'm glad you came," she said. I took her hands without a word; she wrapped her arms around me and nestled into my chest. "Hold me," she said, "just hold me." Then she began to tremble, and slowly I realized she was crying. I held her more tightly, whispering her name over and over, stroking her back and her long blond hair. Her body felt tense as a bowstring. The trailer trembled in the thunder. Lightning exploded all around us, and the air smelled like ozone.

We became lovers with rain hammering the roof, drumming against aluminum, sliding off siding in hissing sheets, steady, sibilant. Thunder crashed relentless as rolling breakers pounding a beach, rocking the trailer to its foundations as Alice and I rocked ourselves to our foundations, and outside everything was lightning flashing and the world went from black to white without transition and then to black again. Water coursed down the roof and the walls of the trailer, coursed down the roof and walls of the mountain, and in the blasting glare of the lightning Alice's breasts looked white and pale. The candle guttered as the wind came damp through the walls low and moaning; the dogs began howling and everything strobed in pulsed light, blue-white, brilliant as thousands of volts, and the whole mountain pounded, pounding, and Alice's body pounded, pounding, rising under mine, her hands under her hips, her back arched into a bow and me kneeling between her legs with my hands on her buttocks pulling her to me, deeper around me. Moving together and moving apart, Alice moaning and the dogs howling, thunder crashing and the trailer rocking, and Alice finally climaxed in a long drawn out cry that silenced the dogs and even the thunder.

Her breathing became moistness, and she collapsed under me, pulling me down tighter into her body moistness, and eventually I fell asleep like that, surrounded by her arms and her legs, her passion and her sexual beauty, her bed and her home and the storm raging outside. But I never did climax. And I slept all night feeling the pain of pelvic bone and cartilage grinding together in a futile attempt at unity. There was a lot I took for granted before I met Alice Bourne.

That night in the trailer I dreamed Alice and I were minks, sleek as the star-studded sky. We lay in our den at the beginning of winter, fragrant dried grass and brown brittle leaves, earth walls close and tunnels narrow, our young just born, and nursing, thriving. Then we were swimming in clear cold water, her silver hair shining, cruising the surface, and sometimes diving—and then a trap caught her leg, her beautiful leg, snapped the bone and held her fast, down under the water. She tried to pull free, bracing three feet on jagged steel, panicking, desperate. She began to gnaw at her leg; bubbles broke around her; she began to drown. I bit *through* her leg and brought her to the surface, my mouth full of her blood, my teeth gentle on the glossy fur of her neck. But she was dead.

Who was the trapper? Through my dream I heard him named by the wind and the water—the low moaning ooou, the sibilant esss. I dreamed of the hunter, the trapper in winter, checking his lines every day in the snow, trudging on snow-shoes, his .22 rifle with its skeleton stock. In my dream I saw his face, his eyes the color of Alice's, his eyes peering down a gun barrel, his gray slouch hat and canvas coat spotted with dried blood, small furs slung over his back. *Louis* the name. *Louis* dragged out slow by wind and rain.

Through my sleep I heard Alice calling *my* name. Ice on the metal roof, sleet and rain and soft wet snow. Outside slashing bursts of lightning still illuminated the night, black trees bare and stark, covered with frozen sleet and hail and glistening, the world icy and wet and everything shimmering.

"Get up, Matt," she said. "Get *up*. We've got to leave." Through the window she showed me the water rising in the hollow, the brook swollen and pregnant, overflowing its banks.

We dressed quickly, by flashlight and lightning—sweaters and raincoats, boots and gloves. I helped her haul the dogs out into the storm, grabbed a blanket and slammed the door shut. As we left a crash came rolling down from the head of the hollow, too liquid for thunder. I paused and tried to see upstream but Alice took my hand and pulled me up the muddy slope behind the trailer. The dogs followed as we slipped and stumbled uphill. A hundred feet above the trailer we reached an old spruce and stopped under its low hanging boughs to look back. In the flashes of lightning a black flood roared heavily down the hollow, tearing out the road and the whole valley floor, trees and mud and rock and water all roiling together. We crouched close under the spruce, the blanket around us, the dogs whimpering at our feet, and watched the hollow purge itself. In one pulse of light the water rose to the level of the trailer, undermining its foundations. In the next the flood tumbled it down.

"Christ, look," Alice said pointing, her cold arm shaking. "I used to play under those." I followed her stare; huge maples all along the brook were crashing down into the torrent. "The dam must have broken." We watched in silence, in bursts of lightning. "Bourne Pond," she said in a monotone. "I used to swim up there." Her voice became trance-like. "Float on my back all summer long—butterflies, birds, hemlocks hanging over the water." Her whole body started shaking then. "All of my life I've walked up the hollow, past those cellar holes, the graveyard, the old sluices and races, up to the mill dam." I held her tightly, but she never stopped shaking; she just became quieter, trembling, staring down at the flood and her history washing away, the hollow scraped clean and raw.

The wind and water still moaned the name. Alice heard it, too; she shook her head slowly, said, "No. Not Louis." And I think that was the first time I felt the sense of doom in Alice Bourne.

When I asked who Louis was, her mouth snapped shut like some steel leg-hold trap, teeth crushing words there like tiny bones. In a sudden flash I saw her eyes narrow in her bruised face, her face as hard as a hunter's. "I kept hearing his name in my sleep," I pressed, trying to read her eyes. "Louis. And in the storm—Louis, Louis." But the afterimage of her face was absolutely unreadable, lifeless and flat, stiff as some drowned otter or mink, a death mask. Blank eyes, old scars and bruises.

I wanted to be back in my house, in my own bed, asleep still. "Who is Louis?" I repeated.

She stiffened next to me. "My uncle," she said, as if that explained everything. "He moved in after my father disappeared." After a moment she said, "He's dead now," and after that she wouldn't say anything more.

I pulled the blanket tighter around us. We crouched together in the freezing rain for a long time. I was as cold as I've ever been, the rain and sleet and snow working down through the spruce onto us, and washing down the mountainside under us, and I felt chilled to my core and wondered if we were to die of exposure there on the side of Bourne Mountain with the dogs crowding around our feet and our wet heat fading. Alice leaned closer to me and I put both arms around her and she was shaking again through cold skin and cloth and I couldn't make her stop.

I felt embryonic. We curled under that wet blanket like twins in a cold womb, waiting for some birth, a stillbirth perhaps, or maybe something worse, something beyond us, some other birth with these floodwaters gushing out of the head of the hollow as if from some huge ruptured amniotic sack and the mountain laboring with thunderous groans, the hollow itself like a birth canal. I began to shiver and my teeth chattered and I wondered what would follow, what would come out of this night, what awful thing would be borne on this flood.

And suddenly I was afraid. I felt the sense of doom in Alice Bourne and I felt it shared now with me and in a flash as brilliant as lightning I understood it was a marriage I was witnessing, not a birth. I was marrying Alice Bourne and I felt a cold darkness descend like a shroud over me and she held me tightly, shaking uncontrollably, and I held on to my fate and my doom, to Alice Bourne, and I wanted to let go and I couldn't let go and she held onto me and I never stopped shivering.

CHAPTER 5

Black Water

Jake

The fire roared, furious, a beast raging so loud in the red brick arch Jake never even heard those two enter the sugarhouse. He heaved the last of the long pine slabs into the sooty incandescence and clanged the iron door shut. On the far side of the boiling pans Alice and Matt already had their coats off and were leaning against the splintered wooden bench, laughing with Patti and holding each other's hands.

Cute. Jake watched them a moment. Alice really *was* cute—long blond body, her face like firelight. Beautiful, actually. A smile so warm he wanted to bask in it. He wiped his hands on his pants and walked over to introduce himself.

Patti had mentioned them before. She'd first met Alice two weeks ago, late February sunset on their raw land. Patti was searching for Jake's cat after an endless day of tapping out, drilling maples along the road that led to Matt and Alice's house site, banging in taps, hanging galvanized buckets and lids. They were putting out six hundred and fifty taps that year, their largest operation so far. Jake had started early that morning with Patti at his side, Brittany on his back, three friends, and the cat. By dusk, only his wife and child remained.

Patti could do anything. Jake watched her welcome Matt and Alice, joking with them, laughing, nursing Brittany at the same time. Patti was a woman of the sixties, and he liked that about her. She wore a headband, no bra, and her black hair hung long and loose. She'd kept some of her weight after pregnancy, though.

Alice wore a ripped wool shirt, loose over a close sweater and tight faded jeans, leather boots. Modern and free and at the same time more bound into that nineteenth-century place than anyone else—firelight and lamplight and a shadow around her. Jake studied her as he approached, trying to understand. When he got close he swept his arm in a wide arc, as if clearing away vapors. "Welcome to the *Many Hands* sugarhouse," he said. His smile creased his beard as he took Alice's hand. "Paradise."

She glanced through the dense steam and smoke. "Paradise?"

"The whole thing," said Jake, continuing to hold her hand. "Let me show you around." Smiling at Matt he said, "Welcome, brother. Make yourself at home." He nodded to Patti, then threaded Alice through the noise and the smell, talking to everyone, laughing, clapping friends on their shoulders. Some were dragging in more wood from the attached shed, others were already restoking the arch fire with six-foot slabs. Jake paused a moment to drain additional sap from the holding tanks into the long boiling pans—this set had been scorched twice already. Stretching up to close the higher valve, he felt Alice stiffen slightly next to him. She stood staring into the corner beyond the cartons of empty tins, attraction and revulsion conflicting in her eyes. Tom Edwards sat there, apart from the others, drinking by himself from his Mason jar.

Jake led her over to the canning table. He drew off finished syrup from the spigot mounted in the lowest corner of the eight-foot pans, and showed her how to test the run for color and sugar content. The syrup poured golden, steaming and thick. Standing near the foaming pans he described how Patti had tended the boiling last night by herself, so he could sleep—he'd been boiling straight for three days and two nights up to that point. Alice nodded, then helped him fill twenty-three tins.

Toward the end of the evening Jake loaded a worn corncob pipe from a bag in his overalls pocket, struck a wooden match on his thumbnail and puffed hard on the pipestem—short sucking bursts—then passed the pipe among the people near him. When it returned to Alice on the third round she took two long dreamy breaths before letting go of it again, and the person who took it from her hand that time was Tom Edwards. He gave her his open Mason jar with a nod and a whiskery smile. She sniffed the rim and he nodded again; she took a sip, then a short hard swallow. Glancing around and licking her lips slightly, she took another swallow, longer, before passing the jar back. Tom licked his own lips, studying her as he raised the jar to his mouth. When he offered it back she took it quickly, tipping her head and pushing her hair out of her face. But Matt came up with her coat then; he touched her shoulder and took the jar from her hand. Then he took her home.

Jake stood alone at the window of the sugarhouse, watching them trudge up the snowy path. Matt was gesturing with his arms, and Alice walked with her head bent, her hands deep in her coat pockets. You're pushing too hard, brother, he thought, rubbing his beard. Nobody can stand that for long.

Eventually they joined hands, and at the crest of the rise, turned to embrace each other. They clung together so tightly and for so long they seemed to merge together. Jake frowned impatiently. No such thing, man. Finally they came apart and started walking again. Jake continued to watch until they disappeared into the night, then he turned away from the window. His friends were all back at their various chores, clanking and roaring and steaming. Patti was rocking Brittany by her crib. Tom Edwards stood near them, swaying slightly on his feet, swaying his way through life, always wanting salvation, thinking a woman could rescue him. He'd never climbed out of his cradle, wanted to be rocked to his grave. Jake sighed, shaking his head, and turned back to the window. For a long time he stood there silently, staring out into the broad night. Later he'd think there should have been more ceremony.

Three times over the next week Jake woke up thinking about Alice. In his first dream he was working in the

sugarhouse, tending to the pans, boiling sap as usual, except
that in the dream he'd been alone. Halfway through stoking the
arch fire he'd suddenly paused, cocked his head to one side,
convinced he'd heard music. But the building behind him was
quiet. Brittany's crib stood empty in the corner, and his coat
hung by itself on a peg over the wooden bench. Jake straightened up, pushed the iron door shut with his boot and crossed to
the window. Then he pulled on his coat and went outside. The
night air was moist with steam and fragrant with woodsmoke.
Jake stared down the path into the dark woods, then followed it
a short way. The sugarhouse glowed behind him with arch fire
and kerosene lamps. Steam billowed into the night through the
roof's huge vents; smoke poured out of the thirty-inch flue.
Wreaths of misty vapor condensed and settled around the
building so thickly that figures appeared within and without,
like wraiths, ghosts in the smoke.

Suddenly Alice was at his side. She didn't walk down
the path or come from the sugarhouse; she just materialized out
of the mist. Her hair was damp and lank, hanging in clumps
like ropes, and her old-fashioned clothes looked thin and worn.
She was shivering, and when he put his arms around her he
realized she was soaking wet. But when he turned to take her
into the warmth of the sugarhouse, the sugarhouse was gone,
and Jake was alone with Alice in the mist and the dark and the
cold woods.

In his second dream they were in his sauna house
together, and he was helping her out of her wet clothes, slowly
unpeeling each dripping garment. He tried to dry her with a
coarse towel, attempting to rub some warmth into her skin. But
the towel turned cold and wet in his hands, and finally he set it
aside. He opened the sauna stove, stoked it and restoked it, and
the room grew hotter and hotter, until finally his eyes watered
so much he couldn't see, until all he could smell was the hot
bone-dry wood of the walls and the ceiling. When he opened
his mouth to speak the burning air scorched his lungs, and
when he tried to breathe, he couldn't.

Alice didn't speak until his third dream, and even then, just three words at the end of it. In that dream Jake was driving home from work, traveling down a crevasse. The roadside snowbanks had grown so high he couldn't see over them—the lights from his truck illuminated only sheer icy walls, pale white, almost blue, slightly glistening. When he got to his cabin, the path there was windswept, trackless, and overhead the stars were all wrong. But his home was well lit; a soft yellow glow from the propane lamps spilled out through the windows, broad swaths across unblemished snow. Jake walked slowly three times around his cabin, then he went inside. The kitchen was warm, warmer than usual, thick and heavy with the smells of unfamiliar foods. Pots simmered on the iron cookstove, but there was no sign of Patti or Brittany. Jake climbed up into the loft to change his clothes. It took a moment to adjust to the dim light above, and he was half undressed before he noticed Alice lying in his bed, watching him. Her body was pale white against the dark comforter, and as she reached toward him her long blond arms seemed almost blue. *Take me then.*

At the end of that week Alice and Matt walked on foot to Jake's sauna house—the road had become impassable with mud, deeply rutted from the hundred-dollar truck that Patti drove back and forth, gathering sap, until it became hopelessly stuck one afternoon and Jake had to dump all three hundred gallons and pull the truck out with the single-cylinder John Deere.

He opened the door to let them into the changing room. The night was light, the weather unsettled March, gusty with warm rain in occasional bursts. Clouds moved fast across the moon's face, and Alice's eyes moved fast across his own face, examining him critically as she stepped across the threshold. Her smile seemed sardonic, her whole bearing cynical.

Matt and Alice had never taken a sauna before, and Jake felt magisterial, ceremonial, conducting the event like a pageant. Halfway through the sauna he reached grandly across the stove, extending a wooden ladle toward the heated rocks at the back. When he tipped the ladle water flowed thinly, a silver stream vaporizing the instant it touched the stones, flooding the small room with a steam so thick and hot it felt like wet weight on his skin. Sweat sprang to his body in a sudden flush.

Patti lay on her back on the lower slatted bench; Matt and Alice lay stretched out on narrow benches above. As the steam cleared Jake found himself comparing the bodies of the two women, the sheen of their skin, the beads of sweat forming on their breasts and stomachs and thighs. Patti's breasts remained swollen from nursing, her legs and trunk still thick from pregnancy, and Jake admired the long lines of Alice's body, the curve of her hips, the hair matted between her pale legs.

On her bench Alice stretched languidly; she met Jake's eyes, watched without flinching, let her own eyes travel up and down his body once, twice, slowly, then met his eyes again and that same mocking smile returned to her face. Jake glanced at Matt, lying on his back with his eyes closed, his body shining in the dim light from the single candle outside the small window. They all were silent together in the dark stifling heat.

Finally Jake asked, "Anyone want a backrub?"

No one spoke for a moment, then Alice said, slowly, "Sure."

"Swap places with Patti then," Jake said and stepped out into the changing room to get the small bottle of body oil. When he returned Alice was lying on her stomach on the lower bench, her head resting on her crossed arms. Jake smoothed oil onto his hands, then traced his fingertips down Alice's spine. He massaged the muscles between her ribs, fingertips curving down her sides, ending slightly further under her body with the completion of each stroke. She stretched full length under his touch, separating her legs a little, relaxing her head into her arms. He kneaded her shoulders and massaged her neck, then drew his hands down the whole length of her body, his fingertips brushing her breasts, her belly, her hips, her thighs. Finally he stepped back, smiling.

Eventually Patti and Alice went outside to cool off. Matt rose and poured more water on the stones. Once more steam rushed up and filled the room, filled them, a hot moist thickness in their lungs. Matt held on to the edge of the upper bench. "Whoa," said Jake, when he could speak again, "I'm going out, too." Matt followed him into the changing room, where the women were already coming in from outside, stamping snow off their bare feet and starting to shiver.

"Cold, cold, cold," Alice said, pressing her legs together and wrapping her arms tightly around herself. Downy blond hair rose up and down the length of her body. Jake smiled, loaded his pipe and offered it to her, but Alice shook her head and followed Patti back to the sauna room. Jake and Matt went out into the blustery night.

Standing naked in the snow, Jake shielded his hands, struck a match and took a deep sucking lungful of sweet smoke before giving the pipe to Matt. He held the smoke for more than a minute, then blew it out in a long thin jet. Finally he asked, "Are you and Alice really going to get married?"

"This spring."

Jake shook his head. "I don't know, man."

"Don't know what?" Matt frowned.

Jake took the pipe back. "I don't think you can plan out life like that." He inspected the bowl, stirred it with a match and relit it. "Things just happen," he said, talking around the pipestem. "Getting married—it's like you think you can predict the future."

Matt laughed out loud. "What the hell are you talking about, Jake? *You're* married."

"Patti's idea," said Jake, drawing in smoke. "She was pregnant." After a moment he began walking toward the brook. Matt didn't follow immediately, and Jake had to wait for him, tapping his foot in the snow. The metal in his hip had begun to ache again, pins and plates—twenty years and four operations later and still he couldn't get used to the way they felt in the cold. Any more than he could ever mute that shrieking futility of skidding tires, crunch of glass and metal breaking. Or forget the sensation of short sudden flight as he left the back seat spinning, up and over his mother screaming, his brother, everything so fast, so fast, and bang, you're dead.

He rubbed his hand up and down his hip. His mother was only twenty-five; already he was two years older than she'd ever grow up to be. When Matt finally caught up to him and said, "Well, that's a good reason," Jake no longer had any idea what he was talking about. "To get married," Matt explained.

Jake frowned, pointing the pipestem at him. "There's no such thing, man. There's no reason for anything. We're just a speck in the universe, my friend, an instant between eternities. Somebody's idea of a joke." He shook his head. "Marriage. Lifetime vows. All those promises. Can't you see how arrogant it is to lay that on someone?"

"How come you're telling me this, Jake?"

"'Cause I think it's true, brother. And I think you need the advice."

"Thanks, Jake. I think you're pretty high."

"High on life, my friend." Do it while you can.

They reached the place where the brook turned sharply, cutting a deep pool against the outside bank. The ice and snow had completely melted there, and the water was black, reflecting the moon. Jake studied the stars; Matt studied the water. "Is that deep enough to dive into?" he asked.

"Yeah, but shit, it's too cold, man. Just roll in the snow." Jake lay down and rolled over quickly three or four times, then sat up, sputtering and wiping his face. Steam drifted up off his body. He sat in the snow with his hands behind him, watching Matt. "Want some advice?" Matt didn't say anything. "Life is for living, Matt. We're all going to be dead before we know it. Marriage." He threw his head back and shook out his hair. "It's not a big deal."

"That's weird," Matt said. He walked over to the edge of the water.

"That's how it is, man."

"I don't want your advice, Jake."

"Yeah, well. Nobody ever does." Jake lay back in the snow, looking up at the moon. "Okay, then—let me tell you a story." He turned on his good side and propped his head on his hand, wondering where to begin. "Tom Edwards—I've known him since kindergarten, and we've been friends ever since. We were on the same Little League team, and later on, the same football team. We learned how to fish together, and how to hunt. Every November we'd spend two weeks with his dad at deercamp—on Island Pond, near the Canadian border." Jake sat up, brushing snow off his shoulder, crossing his legs. "We each got our first buck at Island Pond, both in the same season, the year we turned twelve." He stopped talking for a moment, remembering the big deer in the crosshairs of his scope, pausing to look at him. He could still feel the smooth curve of the trigger, cold metal under his finger, the sudden resistance, then the explosion—the rifle stock smashing into his shoulder and instant death. Bang and it's over. Majesty to meat. Bang and everything's gone.

Matt waited without speaking, half turned away from him. Jake rested his chin in his hands, sighed, and after a moment, continued. "Anyway, we kept a couple of canoes there, and on one of the islands we discovered a cave that nobody else knew about. It was our secret place. Man, we were close. Closer than brothers." He paused, considering. "Then when we were fifteen we both fell in love for the first time. But with the same girl. Lynn played us each along for a little while, then she chose Tom. We had our only fight over that. A hell of a fight. I thought it ended our friendship for good." He let out a long breath, shaking his head. "But Tom had *really* fallen in love. I mean, he was irrational—he was psychotic. Lynn loved him back for a while—just enough—then she dumped him."

Jake stopped talking and leaned forward, scooping some snow up between his hands. He began to pack it together into a dense ball. Matt stood at the edge of the pool, staring down into the black water. Jake studied his back, wondering if Matt had heard anything he'd said. But after a minute Matt asked, "Well? Then what?"

Jake splattered the snowball against a tree trunk. "Tom took it real hard. The next morning he didn't come to school, but I knew where he'd gone. I took my old man's car and drove all the way up to Island Pond—I didn't even have a license then—and I found him in that cave with the muzzle of a deer rifle stuffed in his mouth." Swaying back and forth, rocking and moaning to himself. "He'd been like that for hours. It's not worth it, man. *It's not a big deal.* That's what I told him. I took the rifle and brought him home."

"But it *is*, Jake," Matt said, without turning around. "It *is* worth it."

Jake watched him contemplating the stream, the moon shining on the dark glassy surface, and he shook his head. No, man, it wasn't. He had tried again; there'd been another chance, a girl named Jennifer. But at a college party, a drunken high—a minor fight and Jennifer roaring off with two of her girl friends. *Catch me if you can.*

But all he caught was an image that locked into his memory like a scent, another vision that would return to haunt him for the rest of his life. In the middle of farmland, a rocky pasture—a car on its side and Jennifer half out the window, her long white arms stretched toward him as if she were trying to climb free, as if she were reaching to hold him, to be held. And trickling down one of those perfect white arms a line of blood as fine as tracery, down her forearm to the back of her hand, down the delicate hollow between two tendons there, and over the ring he had just given her, trickling all the way down to the tip of the nail and then, drop by drop, falling to earth.

Her long blond hair was thrown forward over her face and when Jake gently pushed it back there was no mark anywhere, just her startling blue eyes dull white, and her neck at an impossible angle. Bang and you're dead, Jennifer. For hours he sat in that rocky pasture, cradling her, holding her and rocking her.

Jake shivered, looked at Matt and said, "It's going to be cold in there, my friend. It's going to be mighty damn cold for you."

"Not for me, Jake," said Matt, and he dove cleanly into the black water, his white body slicing through the dark liquid like a shaft of light. Bubbles rose and broke at his point of entry. Jake sighed, turned and walked back to the sauna house and the two women inside.

Patti lay stretched out with her back toward the stove; Alice was waiting with her unreadable smile. But it was too cold for Matt to stay in the brook for long, and after a minute Jake went back out after him.

Matt was still in the water. He lay without moving, pale in the darkness, the current rocking him gently, holding him pressed to the bank, like spindrift, driftwood, debris. Jake ran to the edge and hauled him out, laid him on his back in the snow. He pressed his ear against Matt's bluish lips but could barely hear him breathe, the faintest movement of air. Sealing his lips over Matt's mouth and nose, Jake gave him two quick breaths, waited five seconds, then gave him another.

See, man? he thought. See? Just when you think you've got it together, *that's* when it all comes apart. Every fucking time. The biggest joke in the universe. He found Matt's pulse along his cold neck, thready and faint. Rolling Matt's limp body onto his shoulder, Jake struggled to his feet. But when he turned toward the sauna house, Alice stood blocking the way.

"What happened?" she said, touching Matt's face. "What's wrong?"

"Shock."

She took Matt's head in both hands. "He's unconscious."

"He was in the water. Give me a hand." Together they carried him back through the snow.

In the changing room Matt cracked his eyes open as Jake bent over him, rubbing him down with a stiff towel. "Jake," he whispered.

"Take it easy, man. Don't talk."

Matt's eyes slowly closed again. "Don't tell anyone," he muttered, exhaling a long sigh. "It's too stupid."

"All right," said Jake, flicking a glance at Alice. She'd been about to speak, but she pressed her lips together, and quickly stepped back out of Matt's line of vision.

"I owe you one," said Matt.

"It's *all right*, man. Don't worry about it."

Matt's color was slowly returning. After a few moments he pulled himself upright and tugged the towel tight around his shoulders, leaning back against the wall. He sat with his knees drawn up to his chest, resting his forehead on crossed arms, staring at the floor. He shook his head slowly from side to side.

Patti came out of the sauna room, and Alice appeared beside her. Matt looked in their direction. "What happened?" Patti said.

Jake rose and stepped toward her. "Nothing, really," he said. Alice sat down next to Matt and wrapped her arms around him.

Patti went up to him, too. "Christ, Matt, you're blue. What happened?" she repeated.

Matt took a deep breath. "I dove into the brook, that's all."

Patti turned back to Jake, her eyes angry. "And why did you let him do that? Even *you* never do that." She looked disgusted. "He's never taken a sauna before. That was just plain stupid, Jake."

"Damn it, Patti," he said. "I tried to tell him. Three different times I tried to tell him."

Then they were all quiet together. Patti stood apart, her hands on her hips, her mouth hard and frowning. Alice pressed closer to Matt, cradling his head against her breasts. Matt's eyes were shut, his breathing soft and steady, and slowly Alice closed her eyes, too. Then she began to gently rock him, her arms pale white in the dim room, gathering and collecting, and Matt could have been Tom Edwards or even Jennifer. Alive or dead or anywhere in between.

Jake watched a contented smile slowly spread across Alice's face. She must have felt him studying her, because she opened her eyes for a moment, met his, and mouthed the words, "Thanks, Jake."

But he just stared at her, holding her eyes, shaking his head. After a moment he said softly, "There are no saviors, lady, only survivors." And glancing at Matt he could only wonder, are you a survivor, man? You'd better be a survivor.

CHAPTER 6

Hollow Lands and Hilly Lands
Matt

Spring came delicate and raw, full-blown, sudden as ice going out on the river. Overnight new grass transformed the hollow—fragile and lush, astonishingly green—masking the shifting mud, the cycling freeze and thaw. The brook boomed at my feet, still swollen with snowmelt from the mountains, and the air all around smelled rich and damp with earth. Everywhere the world was changing. Leaf buds outlined the crowns of distant trees, blurring horizons transparent as watercolors. Sunlight flooded down crystalline and cold, seeming to illuminate everything. I sat alone in the center of it all, turning the poem over in my head, turning the rings over and over in my hands. Rehearsing.

> I went out to the hazel wood,
> Because a fire was in my head,
> And cut and peeled a hazel wand,
> And hooked a berry to a thread;
>
> And when white moths were on the wing,
> And moth-like stars were flickering out,
> I dropped the berry in a stream
> And caught a little silver trout.
>
> When I had laid it on the floor
> I went to blow the fire aflame,
> But something rustled on the floor,
> And someone called me by my name:

It had become a glimmering girl
With apple blossom in her hair
Who called me by my name and ran
And faded through the brightening air.

The poem was a gift from Alice, left behind that first
night we met, a slim book suddenly on my mantle, green covers
soft and worn, pages opening by themselves to one poem
marked. The words could be taken as a warning I suppose,
some sad prophecy, but they were beautiful words, and it was
beauty I'd chosen to focus on, elegance and image. I read and
reread that poem until I could finally take away my own
meaning, optimism and desire. Today I intended to give those
words back to her, wrap the poem around us both, dress in
Yeats for marriage.

Though I am old with wandering
Through hollow lands and hilly lands,
I will find out where she has gone,
And kiss her lips and take her hands;

And walk among long dappled grass,
And pluck till time and times are done
The silver apples of the moon,
The golden apples of the sun.

The rings were a gift from me. I'd made them myself;
Patti showed me how. I'd tried to inscribe the poem's final
couplet in the two wax patterns—*the silver apples of the moon*
in Alice's, *the golden apples of the sun* in mine. I'd wanted to
join everything. But the words were lost in the wax. When I
made the patterns the etching was too fine; the letters didn't fill
with the sandy investment. After the casting, when I broke
away the gray mold, they had become unreadable symbols.
Now, in the hollow, I inspected the rings. Sunlight glinted off
the highly burnished metal, round smoothness polished perfect

with compound and rouge. Flawless. I kept putting my ring on and taking it off.

Wordless. In an hour I would have to recite the poem out loud, exchange the rings, be married again. But suddenly the lines felt wrong, I felt wrong. I felt restless in the hollow, worse than restless, I felt mute. Every time I tried to say the words, the sense of wrongness increased. Finally I was beginning to appreciate what the poem was really about. I had lived through those stanzas before, was living through them still, their lunatic optimism and obsession. You can't just pick up where you left off.

I didn't want this slow dawning comprehension. I wanted love and passion, ignorance and simple bliss. I needed to be alone—to bury something, I think, to let something go. And there wasn't any time left. "Matt," came rolling down the grassy slope, and I glanced up impatiently. People everywhere want to witness the last moment. But I wasn't really unhappy to see Patti.

"The matron of honor," I smiled. She grinned back with her wonderfully crooked teeth. *Matron* didn't fit her at all—Patti was just twenty-two, surprisingly pretty, long black hair and big dark eyes. "How come you're not with Alice?" I asked. "How's she doing?"

"She's fine. Worried about you. She wanted me to find you." Patti touched my shoulder. "See how you were doing."

"I'm doing okay. Memorizing the poem."

"Are you nervous?"

"Of course." I shivered slightly and wished I had a jacket like everyone else. "How can I help it? Marriage can be like a star exploding." I held the rings out at arms' length, one in each hand, glimmering next to each other. Perfect circles, full of light. One slightly smaller than the other, a moon and sun. "Like a nova: sudden brilliance, fading away to nothing." I cupped the rings in my hands and slid them into my pants pockets. "Like Leslie: a dizzying ascent, an endless fall." I stood up. "Sometimes I think marriage is fatal for a relationship."

"Come on, Matt. Get out of your past." She squeezed my shoulder hard. "You've just got to trust. You know? That's all there is. Look at me and Jake."

"I think trust is something you start out with. Something that gets eroded with time."

She shook her head, and her long hair shimmered, almost metallic, dark blue-black, like gun metal. "It's a leap of faith."

"Into an abyss."

"Jesus, Matt. *Over* the abyss." She sighed. "Do you want to spend the rest of your life reliving your old marriage? Stalled out in Boston at twenty-two? Give it a break."

I ground my teeth and she looked at me closely, then said quietly, "Either way, my friend, it's going to be a self-fulfilling prophecy for you."

"Give *me* a break, Patti. I'm the one getting married here."

She took my hands and squeezed them firmly. "And that's a truly wonderful thing, Matt." Reaching up, she held my head tightly, fingers pressing hard against my temples. Looking right into my face, she whispered, "Open your eyes." She stood on her tiptoes and kissed my forehead. "Alice loves you."

I followed Patti part way up the knoll, but left her near the house site, where people were setting up tables for the reception. I continued alone down into the smaller hollow between the house knoll and the orchard hill, to the footbridge I'd just built across the little brook. Sitting on the rough boards, I noticed a limb had fallen into the water, diverting the current and undercutting the roots of a huge maple on the bank.

I was there only a moment before Mona found me. "I was just talking to Patti," she said, sitting close to me and putting her arm around my shoulders. She hugged me tightly, pressing herself into my attention. Her thick red hair fell over her fine breasts like sleep after lovemaking. Mona had come down from Quebec some years ago; no one knew how, really, except that she came alone. Whenever her past was mentioned, she laid her fingers on the faint white scar running from her cheekbone to the angle of her jaw and smiled thinly—a distant stare came into her dark green eyes and she changed the subject. Mona was a little older than me, but I never knew how much exactly. "You're on in less than an hour, *garçon*. How are you doing?"

"I'm pulling everything together, Mona. Trying to, anyhow." I was quiet for a minute, watching the water undermine the land.

Mona swung her legs over the stream. Eventually she said, "Patti's right, you know. You've got to let go of the past. Give it a kiss, a smile, say *adieu*." She swept her free arm out in the direction of the brook's flow. "Lives are like this, Matt— they just flow on." She dropped a twig into the stream and watched the current start to carry it away. "*C'est la vie*." She turned to me, took my hand and said, "We've all had pain in our lives, *mon ami*. We're not kids anymore."

She leaned closer and I could feel the warmth of her breast against my side, her breath on my neck. I watched the twig get sucked into the eddy behind the fallen limb, spin aimlessly a few times, then sink. *C'est la vie*, Mona. "You're right," I said.

Nothing was ever simple, though, and nothing was ever what it appeared to be. Loving Alice Bourne was a desperate thing, a catching web, an addictive drug. She moved into my house the night we met, and life ever since had been swirling ecstasy with an overarching sense of doom, and I could never get enough.

By early winter we'd merged our dreams—pooled our money and bought some land, designed a home to build together. Two months later the world was snowbound, incestuous, and we'd merged our selves. All of them. It was like falling in love with several people at once. At times it was

exhilarating and occasionally it was terrifying, but mostly it
was just out of control, love and sex and Alice Bourne. It
wasn't something you could ever count on, though. Sometimes
when we made love I'd look into her eyes and someone else
would be there. I'd see past her face to faces beneath—people
I didn't know, people I don't think *she* knew, the endless levels
of Alice Bourne. Sometimes she seemed like an animal, not a
person at all, sometimes a predator, sometimes the prey. And
everything was always all wrapped up within her together, like
time, like her past and my past and our future, all in one instant.
So when Mona would say, *there's only now*, I would agree with
her, but with Mona they were just words, I think.

With Alice Bourne it was real, past and present and
future all at once and all confused—her ghosts and my ghosts,
the two of us now, and all the people we hadn't yet become or
created to outlive us. Sometimes it was beautiful and sometimes it wasn't, and sometimes when we made love those others
came between us. But always there were times when we
connected completely, when I was absolutely lost, hopelessly in
love with Alice Bourne. And those are still the best times of
all, the times that make the most sense, when there is no sense,
when I'm just wrapped up in her arms, and maybe that's what
Mona was trying to mean.

Jake had fashioned circlets of apple blossoms for Alice
and Patti to wear in their hair. He'd made them that morning; it
took him an hour, thick fingers tying the stems together with
sewing thread. Just before the ceremony he ritualistically
placed them, first on Alice's elegant blond head, then on Patti's
shining black one. The women helped each other pin the
flowers in their long hair. "Look at them," he said to me. "Can
you dig it?"

I wore nothing on my head and a wedding shirt on my
back, thick white muslin with two wooden buttons and lots of
blue embroidery. Alice had Patti help make it. A virginal shirt,

although Alice and I were way past that—she had just discovered she was pregnant.

We stood together solidly, the four of us. Alice and I in the center touching, her blue eyes downcast, Jake and Patti on either side, best man and woman. Mona held their child, Brittany, standing next to Michael and Sarah—old friends from Boston who had been present at my first wedding—in the small circle of people surrounding us. We four were like the center of a flower, the core of a fruit. A solid core, a nucleus prior to fission.

The blossoms were already falling. Petals dropped without noise, silent as snow. They fell on Alice's long straight hair, and on the heads and shoulders of the company around us. They drifted everywhere, settling like scattered seed, like fairy dust. Hope or promise. Everyone was quiet, the musicians with their stilled instruments, even the children. It was so silent I could hear the voice of the little brook even though we stood up on the orchard knoll. It was quieter than any church I'd ever been in.

The minister began speaking, but I couldn't hear him. I was back in Boston, four years ago, a dark church all cold stone and naive expectation. I shook my head slightly, as if one could shake off history. I sensed Alice at my side; her strong dry fingers closed around mine. But when I glanced up, I met Sarah's eyes, Michael's; I sank back into Boston, Leslie, time before loss. A time when love was simple and pure, when it glittered with innocence. A time before infidelities, disappearances, compromise. More than anything else, it was trust that was lost somewhere in Boston.

The minister continued talking, his voice deep and penetrating. I squeezed Alice's hand. There's not that much to recommend innocence. Marriage to Leslie was the most expensive lesson I'd ever had in my life, but even so, I still wasn't sure just what it taught. What can we possibly learn from love? And who would even want to try? With Leslie I discovered love's limits, and its limitless cost. How price becomes survival, life itself. Who would ever want to learn that, and what happens when you do? Your past gets poisoned, your present eroded, your future collapses into a time that never becomes. There's plenty of time to be dead when you're dead.

I felt as though I'd been granted a second chance—*if* I could outlive my past, splice it onto my present somehow, mend the broken line of my life. I became conscious of Alice's hand surrounding mine, and of those moments we shared that were transcendent, where there was no past to dwell on, no future to worry about. It made me think *life* could be like that, should be like that—anything less was compromise, a marriage to mediocrity.

Alice squeezed my hand so hard it hurt. I felt her strength course up through my arm, bringing me back to the present. The minister had stopped speaking; he coughed gently. Alice was staring at me. The people surrounding us were very quiet.

"Now Matt will speak a few words," the minister said, sounding like he was repeating himself. The small crowd grew quieter still, all eyes on me now, but I couldn't speak. The words jammed in my throat; the poem seemed suddenly ominous and predictive.

Jake put his hand on my shoulder. "C'mon, man," he whispered. Patti smiled at me with encouragement. I really did try, but when I opened my mouth, nothing came out.

The longer they waited the harder it got, of course, and quieter. I know they all thought I'd forgotten my lines, but I hadn't. I just couldn't say the words out loud. I wondered why I had ever decided to try. The longer I waited the harder Alice's face became, hard as the blue black slate jutting out of the hill behind us. I wanted it soft again, a face I could kiss.

I focused on her hair, her long neck, the curve of her jaw. In my periphery people were shifting from one foot to another. The minister stood frowning slightly, two fingers pushed lightly into his lower lip. Closing my eyes, I breathed in the fragrance of Alice's hair. I took one last deep breath and began to whisper the poem gently in her ear. People stirred impatiently, straining forward to hear, their clothes rustling and annoyance growing. The lines seemed interminable and I felt foolish before I was halfway through. Even whispering I couldn't be sure I would finish. I stopped at the end of the fourth stanza and looked into Alice's face. She smiled, though, and I went on.

In the end a whisper was enough. From the apple trees petals drifted down with the imperceptible breeze. Alice's face softened with her smiles. The wind was so slight it didn't even stir the branches, and the flowers fell softly, quietly, pink to white, succulent, covering the ground like kisses.

Jake passed a joint to me as the reception began, but Patti put her hand on my wrist, shaking her head, saying, "You want to be as clear as you can be. Remember this day for always." Her concern was touching, and I smiled with appreciation. But there are so many different kinds of smiles, and by now I'd used them all. I'd been smiling so much my mouth hurt; it felt like someone else's mouth.

People drifted across the knoll, drinking champagne. Jake had a bottle in each hand every time I saw him, refilling glasses, a foaming fountain, laughing. I'd begun to feel left out. I wasn't drinking champagne myself—I believed Patti was right—and I lagged behind somehow as the whole wedding party lurched forward on a pink and frothy exuberance. Conversations made less and less sense—meaning went to mood, and mood to tiny bubbles exploding.

People were dispersing, some by the brook, a few in the woods, others at the house site. The musicians had split up, and only the flutist was playing now, squatting on the bluff overlooking the large brook. A few couples sat scattered around him, isolated pairs in the May sun. Michael and Sarah lay there, close to each other on the sloping ground between the music and the water, not touching, not talking, just lying next to each other, self-contained, perfect.

As suddenly as if a cloud cut off the sunlight I felt I'd smiled enough, and talked enough, and I just wanted to be alone with Alice. I realized I hadn't seen her for ten or fifteen minutes. It was absurd; this was *my* wedding—I'd been married less than two hours and now she was gone. There was just the poem thudding in my head. I looked all around me but couldn't see her anywhere. I walked past Michael and Sarah with a nod and went in search of her.

I found Patti instead, and when I asked her if she'd seen Alice she just shrugged, sipping champagne, and said, "Where's Jake?"

I walked past several other people, asking the same question, and then went down to the big brook where I came across Tom Edwards, Jake's friend—a neighbor of sorts, who had come uninvited. He sat all by himself, drinking a soda, one of Alice's dogs at his feet. "I think someone went down that path earlier," he said, pointing.

Walking down the track the new foliage obscured everything at first, but then I saw Jake's back, and a woman's arms embracing him. I thought it was Alice and I stopped, wanting innocence now, wanting them to release each other. The scene could be so idyllic, sunlight dappling spring foliage and water glinting and the brook loud. But they continued kissing, and then I saw Mona's red hair over Jake's shoulder. My heart felt leaden; the poem thudded there. Everything felt poisoned, and I ached for Patti; I ached for all of us. But I turned and went back without disturbing them.

Coming upstream the silvery notes of a flute spilled down to me. I walked across the house knoll, smiling and nodding but not really talking to anyone. I went down to the little brook that separated the house site from the orchard hill, sat on the thick planks of the new bridge.

Water swirled around the fallen limb. In one place it rose up a branch and dripped off a little side stem, tiny drops falling like the notes of the flute, splashing, dissolving, washing away. I sat there for a long time, watching the stream. I could be as strong as an oak or one of these maples. As constant as the springhead that gives rise to this little brook. As trusting as Patti. But it wouldn't matter. Things erode. Time is like water.

Looking at the ring on my finger, I thought about my inability to say the poem aloud. I twisted my ring around and around, remembering Patti showing me *her* ring, intertwined branches and berries. The edges were cunningly wrought, and she explained how her ring fit against Jake's, almost nestled within it, forming one whole. "I *made* these," she'd said. "I'll show you how." I'd wanted rings both separate and together, too, but with the meaning of words.

What I hoped for with Alice was transcendence of time; and maybe that's what hope itself is—that instant of belief, that denial of history. Maybe that's what love is. Or what I wanted it to be. It was no surprise that I couldn't say the poem out loud, or that the words never emerged on the rings. We grope around wordless. I'd taken everything out of a larger context.

I watched the water pass under the bridge without really seeing it go by. When I did finally notice it, I saw petals of apple blossoms drifting down on its surface, and suddenly I knew just where Alice was.

I climbed the hill to the orchard knoll, plucking a blossom at the first tree I passed. I snapped and pulled the thick stem, bent like an arthritic joint. It only broke halfway, the dry gray bark flaking off at the break and bending into close ridges at the hinge. The outer wood was all wet and green, the inner wood bone white. I twisted the twig against my thumb-nail and pulled it free.

Alice had already taken off her crown of flowers. When she saw me she smiled but didn't speak. I walked up to her and with my index finger softly lifted some hair from over her right ear, and gently threaded the stem of the blossom among the blond strands. It glimmered there, pale white and pink, next to her eyes and smile. She turned her face up to me, her eyes reflecting the blue Vermont sky. And my love and hope. I kissed her eyes so gently, my lips as delicate as flower petals; I kissed her forehead harder and then her mouth very hard and I pulled her face next to mine, her body against my chest. I held her so tightly nothing could ever come between us.

CHAPTER 7

The Lemon Fair

Matt

Dawn breaks over the Lemon Fair as sure and certain as the river itself, still light on still water collecting, pooling deep below the ruined dam as it gathers itself for the long easy run down the valley. I slide our canoe into the river by the mossy foundations of a vanished mill, broken walls rising vaguely through the water, early morning river fog obscuring everything. Vapor spirals drift across the surface like ghosts, and ghosts have come between us.

"We're ready," I say. "Hop in the front."

Alice stands frowning, her hands on her hips. "Too small," she says. "I'll sit in the back."

"You'll have to steer from the stern."

"I can do that."

I stand sighing, shaking my head. "Alice," I say softly, almost to myself. For nearly three months I'd been trying to understand. I study her face and her body, searching for some sign, some change I could see. But Alice's pregnancy is a private thing, fundamental shifts all deep within her. And as she stands there looking down the river I realize I don't know how to touch her anymore. Even yesterday's lovemaking already feels like a dream, only *my* dream. "You don't know anything about canoeing," I say finally.

"You could float down this river on an inner tube," she says, and she is right. Below the dam the Lemon Fair is stillwater for miles, all the way to its confluence with the Roaring Branch, and even after that it continues broad and easy, occasional Class II whitewater at the most, until it reaches the covered bridge spanning the gorge at Wardsboro.

But the river is incidental. Mostly I want to preserve the mood from yesterday, so I concede. "Okay. You take the stern. But when we get to the first whitewater we'll have to pull out and switch places."

"I'll steer the canoe," Alice says, and then she is silent.

I push us off. The canoe slices silently across the placid surface, carried by current; I rest my paddle across the wooden gunnels and peer into the dark water ahead of us. Fog drifts slowly across the water and birds begin to call from both banks and directly overhead. We glide through misty sound as dawn slants across the sky above us, illuminating just the hilltops on the western shore. Alice steers from the stern, never saying a word, and I sit in the bow, suspended over the river, a point without time.

This is a celebration trip for us, Alice's idea, a break from housebuilding, a marker as definite as the small topping-off evergreen I'd nailed to the ridge pole when the house frame was finished. The rapids at Wardsboro are miles away and the river is peaceful and still. I stow my paddle and let my hands drift in the water, fingers lightly brushing the surface. The last time I was on the Lemon Fair I was alone, and I'd heard a kestrel calling, his shrill *killy killy killy*, searching for his mate. The line of sunlight creeps lower down the western hills and starts to spread across that side of the valley floor. The mist continues rising and still there is no sound from Alice behind me, just the birdsong along the river; I feel alone on the water and not even a part of things, just barely touching the surface of the river, skimming the Lemon Fair with my fingertips.

In the stillwater with the fog around me, the world wet and gray and indistinct, I think of Leslie, the ghost between us. It's not a choice I have; it's more like a punishment. Incarcerated in our old Boston apartment, condemned to repeat those nights where every car parking, every door opening, every footstep on the hallway stairs was never Leslie returning. I'd wake and drink coffee, smoke cigarettes, wait. Listen to the dark. *I'm not the one who started this Matthew.*

Leslie was my first lover, my only lover, what more can be said? I can see her so clearly—dark hair falling loose as she curves over her guitar, fingers delicate and fast, her eyes as dreamy as the songs that well up from somewhere deep inside her, somewhere I used to know, songs of love and home and family. Leslie. My first wife, my best friend, my only lover.

We were just seventeen when we married, but we never fell into that teenage pregnancy trap, WIC programs and social workers. I'd seen what had happened to my mother. Leslie and I earned scholarships to college; as soon as we graduated from high school we moved to Boston.

Where part of me still remains, shackled to a halted time, the broken wall, trust leaking out everywhere. So that sometimes, even now, when I hold Alice close to me, I embrace Leslie instead. And when we should be most intimate—when Alice and I make love and I can close my eyes at last—it's Leslie I want to be holding, Leslie I want to return to, that lost time of trust.

On the back streets of Boston stands a place in my life, a stone-gray club I've only entered twice—once to betray Leslie, and once to lose her. I still can't comprehend what happened there. Although I've come to understand that everything we do is ultimately our own free choice, still, those two evenings feel like they happened to somebody else. When I entered that club the first time, it was just to kill an hour. But killing is a thing without limits, and sometimes, I think, the only thing I'm good at.

When I crossed that threshold a brown-eyed girl turned from the polished bar with a face so warm and inviting I had to smile back. Her look was so expectant and her smile so purely for me that when she gestured to the place at her side I barely hesitated. I went right up to her, and there were no boundaries at all, no limits or walls, just the scent of her body, the swell of her breasts, swirling soft fragrance and heat. She was just waiting for me, simply offering herself to me—no woman had ever done that before. I was twenty-two years old. In my whole life I'd never known any other woman than Leslie. I was over my head, but after we touched I didn't care. I went home with the brown-eyed girl. It was like drowning.

That was my only infidelity in five years of marriage, and I should have kept it to myself. But it affected me more than I ever dreamed it could, and Leslie noticed the change in me. *Trust me* she said *tell me*. There was a traitor in my heart, a saboteur hidden there my whole life, waiting to poison everything. *Talk to me* she said. *Tell me.*

I still don't understand why I ever did. Maybe I thought I could expiate sin with confession, that honesty could reverse betrayal. But mostly I think I was asking for forgiveness, reversal, as if Leslie could undo what I'd done. That was before I understood the fragility of things, the limits of love, that Leslie was human.

The moment I told her she started to wail, an endless animal sound, monochromatic gray. I never want to hear that sound again, like a heart torn out, mortal and final and absolutely without hope.

Still, for months afterwards, I thought we'd survived that wail. Five years is a long time, and our life seemed to return to a normal course. I made a vow then that I've never broken since—that I would marry loneliness before I'd betray someone who loved me. I'd build walls to contain love, walls so strong that nothing could leak out, no stranger could get in.

But timing is everything. Within that same year we'd returned to those back streets of Boston, Leslie demanding to visit that stone-gray club, and the only plausible explanation is she already knew the man she was to meet there that night— that she'd set up that evening's events beforehand. She'd always had this need for symmetry and closure.

We'd had a couple of drinks together and were dancing on the crowded floor when the man with the red beard came up alongside us, bobbing and weaving, then dancing with Leslie, and when I wanted to go back to our table she said *go ahead I'm going to dance* and later when I wanted to go home she said *go ahead I'm going to dance* and when I argued with her she said *I'm not the one who started this Matthew.*

And that night she didn't come back. The next day I called our friends looking for her, and although they all had lots of questions not one had any answers and finally I made the last call I wanted to make, I called her parents. I tried to sound casual when I said hello, but Leslie's mother said straight off *she can't talk to you today maybe tomorrow give her some space Matt she's been through a lot.*

And the day after that Leslie's mother said *she'll call you back give her some space,* and I waited all day by the telephone and I waited all night and finally I couldn't stand it, I called her parents' house around midnight; I woke them all up and Leslie's mother said *you're just making things worse Matt she needs to be alone she's been through a lot.*

Two days later they still wouldn't let me talk to her, and I drove from Boston to her parents' house. Her father met me at the door and wouldn't let me inside. And the second time I drove to her parents' house her father said *she's not here anymore she'll be in touch.*

But the one who eventually got in touch was her lawyer.

Touch. Connection. This endless hunger for love. Thinking about it in the months that followed I realized the want was there for as long as I could remember. It went all the way back to the time my mother and I moved into John's house, when I shot the Thompson kid with the arrow, then ran away.

This bottomless hole of want, deep and dark and limitless as the old quarry I used to swim in as a boy. The still pool so beautiful on the surface, sheer marble walls gray-white and the water like black glass, but no one remembered how deep it was, just that the bottom was littered with derricks and cranes pushed over the edge when the quarry closed a century ago, and that a boy once dove straight down from the highest wall and was never seen again, his body still down there, impaled on some jagged rusty spear in the depths, the water so deep and dark that even the state police scuba divers couldn't recover him.

I start to paddle quietly. I leave tiny whirlpools each time I pull my paddle out, water moving in to fill the space left by my blade. There is a pressure in my chest, an ache in my lungs, as though I can't breathe. In the shallows at the edge of the river a great blue heron stands in the misty vapor, pale and skeletal, and we are silent, drifting down the deep river, the current strong and the surface placid.

The water in the Lemon Fair is high for midsummer, and we slide downstream at a fair pace through its calm upper reaches. Sometimes we drift near the bank and I can see sunfish fanning their tails over their nests in the shallow water. Still not a word from Alice in the back of the canoe. Our mood from last night is fragile at best; I don't want to risk damaging it. Yesterday was so fine—we'd finally closed the house to the weather, not too far behind schedule, and afterwards made love for the first time in more than two weeks, and without a long discussion beforehand.

Alice Bourne. Over and over she'd say *Not tonight, I'm too tired. Not this morning, I've been sick every morning since I became pregnant. Not this afternoon. Tomorrow. Tomorrow. Tomorrow.* In the space of not much more than half a year we'd fallen from ecstasy to argument, summoned some monster lurching from the deep. And neither of us knew how to contain it, where it came from exactly, or how to send it back.

I listen to the silence behind me. I feel like Orpheus, leading us out of the underworld, forbidden to look back. I can't step away from her need for space. Cycles repeating, connection and rejection. I can't accept her distance with any kind of grace. Call it connection, but what it's really about is that desire for wholeness, that limitless want satisfied, and waking up in an embrace.

Gradually the sun clears the eastern hills entirely, and we are bathed in light, surrounded by bright sparkling water and about to enter the first minor riffs where the river widens and the land begins its steady drop toward Wardsboro. I turn around and Alice is still there of course, calmly steering us through the easy rips. "You are such a beautiful woman," I say.

"Thanks."

"How're you doing, lady?"

"Okay, Matt," she answers, her right hand on the gunnel, fingers spread across varnished wood, lightly bracing her paddle against the hull, easy stern rudder. And the world really seems easy, early morning and warming sun and gently rolling water. The sound of birdsong gradually fades away. "What were you thinking about up there?" she asks. "I thought you'd fallen asleep."

"About loving you yesterday, curling up next to you afterwards."

"Yeah, that was nice," she says. "I wish it were like that more often." And then she is quiet again, drawn into the totality of her pregnancy, her self-contained immediacy, that perfect, mysterious union: pregnant woman.

"It *could* always be like that."

She looks no different than she always has, but she is on the other side of a wall. "I don't think so."

"What do you mean?"

"You carry too much baggage around, Matthew."

"What are you talking about?"

"You've never gotten over your old marriage. You wake up with it every day, and now I do, too."

Distance escalates. "That's not true," I say.

"It sure is. It's like you're trying to pick up where you left off. I'm not going to be turned into someone else, Matthew." Her fingers tighten around the paddle's grip as she digs the blade deeper into the water.

After a moment I say, "Look, Alice. *You're* the one creating the distance. Ever since you've gotten pregnant you haven't wanted to make love."

"Yeah, well, lovemaking's not as simple as it used to be. Turn around and start paddling."

After the confluence with the Roaring Branch the speed of the river increases considerably, and the valley floor narrows again, dropping off as we move closer to the rapids at Wardsboro. The heavy rains of early summer have raised the height of the river, and this section, usually easy riffles, is broken water as far as I can see—rocks tear the surface, and new chutes and holes have formed in places usually flat. As we enter the whitewater Alice calls "left" and "right" and I haul the bow around obstructions, dig hard, pull us clear.

In a short stretch of flatwater I turn around and say, "The river's higher than I thought."

"No problem."

"We should pull out, change places."

"I can do this myself. Keep paddling."

"Christ, Alice, you don't have any idea what you're doing."

"Hard right, Matthew. Pay attention."

On this section of the river quartzite boulders litter the banks and the bed, and the surface is rough in places where it barely conceals ledges. Occasional boulders break through the water and the river churns white around them, forming boiling eddies and holes. Alice guides us smoothly past a dozen rocks, but where two rise close the current accelerates into a narrow chute and even though I pull our bow sideways as hard as I can, we slide broadside into the first rock, broach the canoe and barely scrape past the second. I turn around and shout, "Pull out over there," pointing with my paddle.

"No," she shouts back. "I'm doing fine." Still I don't want to argue. But the current increases and so does the whitewater, and I'm not always effective steering from the bow, especially since Alice's stern rudder doesn't make intuitive sense. We aren't good at communicating our thoughts, coordinating our actions, or reading the river.

We scrape by another rock and twice grind hard over ledges just below the surface. Once more I try to persuade her to pull out, and once more she refuses. "We've made it this far," she says, as if I should congratulate her.

Instead I try to pull us to shore from the bow alone, but then we enter a place where boulders stretch thickly from bank to bank and I have to concentrate on the best way to bring us through. I turn again. "Bring us left a little, and we'll shoot past the right of that flat rock." But Alice shakes her head no, nodding to the right; she steers us too hard in that direction. The canoe begins to slide broadside to the current again. I pull hard off the left bow to straighten us out and we almost make it, but we slew sideways, ship water and flip.

Both of us are upstream from the canoe, which is full of water now and pressing into the rocks with all the weight of the river behind it. We stand up waist-deep in the rapids, bracing ourselves with our paddles and supporting each other. I take the bow line and we make our way to the shore, boulder by boulder. Then I go back for the canoe.

When I finally manage to drag *it* ashore, we have our first real argument of the day. And like so many others, this one comes down to position and command, competence and control. Who is going to navigate. Who is going to steer. Alice is adamant. "Look Matthew, *I* can do it. I've brought us this far, and I'll take us the rest of the way."

I change my approach. "You're pregnant," I remind her.

"If I can help you build a house, I can certainly go canoeing."

"But these are real rapids now."

"I can take care of myself, Matt."

When we leave the shore Alice is still in the stern, but at least we've agreed to work together, communicate commands. I would navigate; she would steer.

A mile above the bridge at Wardsboro the water becomes consistently frothy, broken rips from shore to shore, and I stop thinking about Leslie and Alice and become absorbed in water and rock. "I've got the hang of it," Alice shouts, and we travel the last stretch quickly, competently.

And soon are approaching the pullout above the rapids. "Left," I call over my shoulder. But Alice doesn't hear me, or maybe she deliberately ignores me. We continue straight—then move out toward the center of the river. I turn and shout, "Alice. Bring us to shore." Once more the canoe starts to slew broadside to the current.

"Paddle, Matt," she shouts back. "Hard." And I have no choice but to straighten us out.

This is crazy. "Pull over to the bank," I demand, and I try to force us over with a bow pry, but she compensates from the stern and I can't match the efficiency of her position there. Ahead of us the first large chute starts to form, and once we're in that we're committed. "Alice, don't be stupid."

"Hard right," is all she answers and then we are in the chute, in the rapids, past the limits of our ability and our last chance to pull out. We hit a rock hard and curve around it; a large wave breaks over the side, soaks me and floods the canoe. Immediately it becomes as heavy as stone, impossible to steer. The bow hits another rock and we jam sideways. "Right. Hard right," Alice shouts, but there is no water under me anymore, just the curving hull and rock and I wedge my paddle between them, haul down on the shaft and manage to lever us off. At once the river claims us, sucking us straight in. "Right. Left," Alice shouts, not making any sense at all, and then we are through that flume and into a hole slipping fast and broadside again. Water piles up behind us, smashes us sideways onto a sloping boulder, and for an instant our canoe just hangs there, as if it were beached—as if we could just stand up, step out, walk away. Then the boat shudders and starts to pivot, the bow slowly swinging upstream. I swear at the rocks, the river, Alice. I jam my paddle down again, haul on the T-handle with both of my hands and all my strength and the bow moves back a little. Somehow Alice manages to bring the stern around and for a moment I think we might make it but then the shaft of my paddle snaps and then everything is hopeless. We slam back against the rocks and the river rolls us; water pours over the gunnel in a flood and we tip and swamp and capsize all in a second.

Then there is just water and rock and nothing to breathe. Pinned between the hull and a boulder I try to locate Alice but everything shifts, the boat crushes my shoulder and noise is predominant, noise and water. Noise most of all, and water like a wall, smashing me down. There is an instant when I come up futilely clawing, fingers slipping off the curved hull, the canoe broadside to the river and full of its water and current, pressing me against the rock, cracking my ribs and pinning me there, then it grinds around me, scraping my chest across a boulder, a huge blast of pain quickly transcending to numbness. And then the current has me, sucking me down, noise and water and the inexorable pull of the river itself, the embrace of the Lemon Fair. I try to hold onto rock but it is impossible and I am smashing my way through the rapids in the grip of the river, water and air and water, holding my breath and coughing where I can, trying to breathe, swallowing the river, the roar, and the rocks exploding.

I come to the surface in a deep still pool at the foot of the rapids. My chest is numb, my shoulder is throbbing, and I can't see Alice anywhere. I spin through a quick circle, shouting her name, but the banks are empty, and downstream the swamped canoe is empty. I take as deep a breath as I can manage and dive to the bottom, scrabbling around with my hands, my eyes stinging from silt and my lungs pounding. I surface for air and dive again and the third time I rise I hear Alice call my name and then I see her halfway up the rapids, way off to the right, picking her way to shore.

I swim to her side of the river and crawl up onto the bank, then limp upstream and reach her just as she walks out of the water. I can't speak, but she looks all right, and she nods to affirm that. I touch her shoulder, take her in my arms, draw her to my chest, scraped and bloody; I draw her to me as hard as I can and we sink to the ground at the edge of the Lemon Fair. For a while we just sit there, holding each other. And when she says *Matthew I'm sorry*, I answer, "Yeah, well, it's okay." It's hard for me to talk. I take a deep breath. "We've made it this far," I point out, then I don't say anything more.

CHAPTER 8

Chimes

Alice

Standing up quickly made Alice dizzy, and she closed
her eyes, swaying a little as the world spun. She put a hand to
her forehead, a hand on her belly, nausea sour in the back of
her throat. Patti's voice continued without pause, though,
disembodied in the shimmering heat. "No, it wasn't like that at
all. We made love the whole time, actually."

Alice swallowed twice, cautiously drew unsteady
breath. When she opened her eyes there was only brilliance.
"But not your first trimester."

"First, second, third—right up to the end. I don't think
I was as sick as you were, though." Patti squatted among deep
blurry green, full sunlight shining off her blue-black hair, long
and loose. For the moment, just her face: light glinting off
teeth and eyes and crooked smile. And words coming out of
swirling heat, coming out of nothing like living things, bright
birds in air, fish flashing in water. "Are you okay?"

"More or less."

In the garden they were harvesting tomatoes, twisting
vines and breaking stems, the acrid fragrance overwhelming.
Patti's garden was vast: raised beds and ordered rows, peren-
nial groupings ranked like soldiers—her structure imposed on
her world. Garlic and marigolds edged the perimeter; gladiolus
and dahlias defined the center path. Patti's vegetables stretched
out straight for a hundred feet before stopping at the compost
pile next to Jake's rusting bus. Her tomatoes were small, plum-
sized, deep red—early varieties with names like *Arctic Ice* and
Canadian Wonder. Alice's garden tomatoes were four times
the size of Patti's, but still green, hard as leather, hopeless now
at the end of summer—September's frosts sudden and final.

79

"Did it hurt?" Alice asked, pushing hair back from her forehead.

"Hurt? No, Jake is very gentle."

"Not Matt." She took a deep breath and moved her hands to her hips. "When I told him how heavy he was—how much it hurt—you know what he did? He started to take me from the back. Like a dog." A thief in the night.

"Hmm," Patti said, frowning. "Personally I like that position."

"So does Matt. But I need to see his face."

"You guys should talk about that one." Patti was sorting tomatoes as she picked them, turning each one over in her hand, placing perfect tomatoes in one basket, slightly blemished ones in another. Anything worse she threw over the fence into the pasture.

Alice began to pace up and down between the rows. "And he whispers in his sleep. That's the part I really hate. The other night we had this long argument about not making love. We weren't talking when we went to bed. Matt fell asleep, but I couldn't." She paused in front of Patti and lowered her voice. "He got hard in his sleep, and I took him in my mouth—I'd never done that before—but when he was ready to come he started whispering *Leslie, Leslie.*" Suddenly her mouth tasted sour again. "I still can't believe it. There I am, carrying his child, sucking him off, and he's dreaming away. Whisper-ing, calling me *Leslie.*"

"Jesus." Patti stopped picking tomatoes. She squatted on her heels, looking at Alice.

"*Jesus* is right. I slapped him out of *those* dreams." Lost in some memory, some ecstasy, *Leslie.* "I'll never do that for him again."

"Wow," said Patti, shaking her head. "Yeah. It's different with us." She stood up with her two baskets of tomatoes. "You should come inside."

By the kitchen door wind chimes hung still in the heat, and Alice set them in motion as she entered the cabin, brushing the silver cylinders lightly with the tips of her fingers. She'd made the chimes herself, last winter's present for Jake and Patti. Matt had found the narrow aluminum conduit, and Alice had cut and drilled more than a hundred different pieces of tubing, experimenting with length and tone. Gradually she'd used up her whole supply, and still she wasn't satisfied with the relationship between size and sound. Matt had to make a second trip for more material, and that night he asked her, "What are you looking for exactly?"

She sat cross-legged among a litter of rejected silver pipes. "Perfect notes."

"What's wrong with some of these?" He selected a tube randomly from the debris around her, held it suspended by its nylon line and struck it with a wooden block. A clear tone rang out. "*This* one sounds perfect—what more do you want?" He reached for another.

"They have to be just right," Alice said patiently. She took the first cylinder from him, struck it herself, listened critically, struck it once more, then put it back on the pile of discards. "Perfect notes. Perfect harmony." She sat back on her heels. "What I *want*, Matthew, is for them to sound like love."

"They don't have to be perfect to do *that*," he said. But he went out of the room and left her alone.

Eventually she was satisfied with the sounds she could construct, and she fashioned strikers from polished wood, fired spoon-shaped pendants of thin clay to catch the wind, then joined everything together with strong monofilament. She assembled a second set of chimes for her own house, and another for her friend Mona; she'd even given a set to her neighbor Liza.

By the kitchen door Patti set down her baskets of tomatoes, reached up with both hands and silenced the chimes. "Brittany's finally asleep," she explained. "She had colic again last night."

"Sorry," Alice said, turning in the narrow doorway.

Patti's kitchen had no running water so Alice washed tomatoes in a bowl on the plank table while Patti sterilized jars in the speckled pot on the iron cookstove. The kitchen was hot even before she built the wood fire, and after they put the tomatoes on Alice wandered out into the new addition, still just an open frame, post and beam, no sheathing yet. Jake had rigged a tarp over some cross timbers, shading Brittany sleeping in her playpen. "Shh," Patti said, coming in behind her. "Let her sleep. Jake was up with her again all last night."

Alice moved quietly around the open space, admiring the joinery of the beams. "Look at these," Patti said softly. She ran her hand over an intricate union between two horizontal timbers. "Jake calls them scarf joints." Alice studied the way the huge beams met, interlocking hands holding the entire frame together. The total structure was like that, everything locked and interlocked by function and form, held together without any nails or fasteners. "Jake says you could roll this whole thing down a mountain, and when it got to the bottom it would still be square and true." Alice looked up through the hexagonal roof timbers, like looking out through the bleached bones of a whale, a skeleton in the sky.

On the stove tomatoes rose bumping through boiling water. Patti scooped them out with a large perforated spoon, dipped them into cold spring water and their skins burst, split and peeling. Alice stripped them and packed them into steaming Mason jars. "You can take all of these," Patti said. "I never did like canned tomatoes." She damped down the fire in the Waterford stove, but the kitchen just grew gradually hotter, punctuated with popping as the jar lids formed seals.

"Let's go down to the brook," Alice suggested for the second time. "It's cooler there."

"All right," Patti said. She gave Brittany a final check, and the two women followed the path out to the road, past it to the sugarhouse and the sauna and the brook just beyond. Near the deep pool where the brook turned they took off their sneakers and sat on the bank, close to each other, their feet in the water.

"You guys are lucky," Alice said, after a moment.

"Yeah, we are." Patti was dipping her toes in the slow current, and the dark water curled a little, eddying lazily around them.

"You're lucky to have Jake," Alice said, turning to look at her.

"Well, he's lucky to have me," Patti answered with a smile.

Alice looked down at the water for a moment, trying to see below the surface. "But—I mean he's perfect."

"Nobody's perfect, Alice."

"You know what I mean. He's as close as they come."

"Nobody comes close," Patti said, laughing. "And that's okay." She spread out a blue blanket on the slope behind them. They took off their shorts and T-shirts and stretched out in the sun. Lying there naked, Patti turned to Alice. "You're starting to show a bit."

"I can feel her now." Feel the new life forming inside, separate from the rest. Another chance. Alice lay on the bank and studied Patti. Was there something special about Jake? Or just something wrong with Matt? She closed her eyes and turned her face to the sun. Probably there *was* something special about Jake. "You're lucky to have him, Patti," she said again.

How *did* she end up with Jake anyway? How does one end up with anybody? Was it always chance, coincidence so common it became an embarrassment later? One went to buy groceries, wash laundry, rent a room—and suddenly life was defined forever by some accident, some happenstance, some man. But then there were people like Mona. Mona didn't need men; Mona was a person apart. She'd outgrown men, evolved past that; she was a whole woman.

Patti reached over and touched her shoulder. It took Alice a moment to understand Patti was talking about herself, her other half, and had been for a while. "It's like I grew up suspecting something was missing, but never knowing what it was exactly." She rolled on her side and looked into Alice's face. "It's not that I'm needy." She stopped for a moment, searching for words. "It's more like everything was okay—you know, *just* okay—until I met Jake, and after that things finally started to make sense. I could have gone on without Jake—it would have been all right. But with Jake everything really fit."

"Was it like that for him?"

Patti looked at her in surprise. "Sure. Of course."

"You're lucky," Alice said once more, touching Patti's arm. After a moment she continued, "It sure is different with Matt." She drew in a long low breath. "No matter *what* I do, it's never enough." Sighing, she pushed herself into a sitting position. "A hundred times I've told him, *I'm on your side*— but anyone who tries to love Matt becomes automatically suspect. He simply can't trust another human being. He's always testing, always doubting—always expecting the worst. And someday he's going to make that happen." Alice sat with her elbows on her knees, her chin in her hands, long blond hair framing her face. "*No* woman could ever give him enough. And even if she could, he wouldn't be able to accept it." She looked away over the brook. "It's like he's on the other side of a wall all the time. Like I'm throwing my love against a wall, and it all runs down splashing, washing away." She shook her head. "And none of it ever touches him, never, not one single drop."

Patti was just watching her with a slight frown. She didn't say anything. Suddenly Alice felt exhausted. Ever since she'd become pregnant she was tired all the time. Once more she lay down. Patti took her hand and Alice closed her eyes. The air smelled of ferns and dry leaves and the sunlight was welcome on her body. She felt warm and safe next to Patti, and began to doze off. Through her thickening sleep she heard Patti say, "Don't worry. You'll be all right. Things will work out." And she fell asleep wondering what the world would be

like if there were just women, a planet without men. Just
women, helping each other raise children, grow food, can
tomatoes for winter.

She awoke to pressure from Patti's hand and the sound
of Jake's voice, "Wow. Two beautiful women naked in the
woods."

She sat up and reached for her clothes. "Turn around,
Jake. I want to get dressed," she said.

"Don't trouble yourself on my account," he grinned.
He knelt behind Patti and began massaging her shoulders.
Smiling, he watched Alice pull on her shorts and T-shirt.
"Wood nymphs."

"Did you check Brittany?" Patti asked.

"She's fine. Sleeping like a baby." Jake stretched out
on the blanket where Alice had just been. The air wasn't so
still anymore—a slight breeze wafted warm through the trees.
"Paradise," he said, to no one in particular.

"I'm going to wake Brittany," Patti said, dressing.
"It's time for her lunch."

Jake and Alice watched her walk up the path. "She's a
good woman," Alice said.

"That and more," Jake answered, but he wasn't
watching Patti—when Alice glanced down at him he was
looking up into *her* eyes, and he continued to look, smiling.
Alice returned his gaze for a second, then looked away. "Still,
she's not everything," Jake added.

"But she *is* your wife, Jake," Alice said, looking at him
again. "*And* my friend."

"My friend, also—just like you. It's all different and
the same." They continued to contemplate each other. Alice
began to feel awkward standing but she didn't want to lie down
again, so she sat on the edge of the blanket opposite Jake, her
legs crossed, her back curved a little, her arms in her lap. Jake
turned on his side. "Our being friends doesn't hurt Patti.
We're not taking anything from her."

"I don't know."

Jake moved a little closer and rested his head on a propped elbow. He kept smiling and looking in Alice's eyes. She felt her face flush. She didn't see him extend his hand, just felt his fingertips on her leg, lightly on cloth, the outside of her thigh. Her eyes widened involuntarily but she didn't move her leg. "Love isn't something you run out of," he said. He ran his fingertips gently down onto her skin. "It's there for the having." He began to increase the pressure of his fingertips; began stroking with his whole hand, slow sliding arcs up and down her leg, gradually moving toward her inner thigh. Alice suddenly uncrossed her ankles, straightened her legs, rolled over onto her stomach and her body's new discomforts. She rested her head on her crossed forearms.

"Don't," she said.

After a moment Jake knelt at her side and began to massage her shoulders, softly at first, then more firmly. "People want to connect, but they never let themselves." He slid his hands down her sides, his thumbs along her spine, fingertips just brushing her breasts. Alice felt the swelling there, her nipples becoming erect. "Why not face up to it? All it ever comes down to is human connection. The most natural thing in the world."

Jake massaged the small of her back, her buttocks and hips, her thighs and calves, and Alice shifted her body slightly under the pressure of his hands, murmuring. But when Jake slid his hand up the inside of her thighs, she rolled away from him, sat up, drew her knees to her chest and wrapped her arms around her legs. "You're married to Patti."

"That I am."

"I'm married to Matt."

"So what?" Jake slid toward her and wrapped his arms around her folded form. "Your friend Matt is a romantic. You know what I mean? He'll never be happy, regardless." Alice felt off balance against his chest. "There is no end to his want, see? You'll never satisfy him. He's looking for a savior but there isn't any." When Jake tried to kiss her she pressed her lips together, turned her face and body away. Her skin was flushed—she could feel its heat and a thin sheen of sweat, and she could tell Jake felt it too. She broke his embrace and stood up, swaying slightly.

Jake looked at her. He ran his hand through his hair. "You know what people regret at the end of their lives, Alice?"

She shook her head.

"Nothing," he said.

"Well, I'm not at the end of my life yet."

"You never know that one ahead of time." Jake stood also, hooking his thumbs in the back pockets of his jean shorts. "Do you know what there is at the end of life?"

Water, Alice thought. Ice and water.

"Dust. That's all there is. Dust." Jake studied her for a moment without speaking, then turned and, still not saying a word, started up the path toward his home, his wife and child. As he moved away his gait seemed fluid, confident—Alice watched his swinging arms, his rhythmic hips, the muscles rippling across his broad shoulders. He didn't look back.

After a moment she followed, feeling the need to say good-bye to Patti. Besides, it would appear odd not to collect the jars of tomatoes. But where the path crossed the narrow road Alice paused, filled suddenly with an overwhelming desire to just leave, and she had to force herself to continue. Approaching the last bend in the path she heard her wind chimes by the kitchen door, and for the first time she really noticed the weather was changing. From the bend she had a clear view all the way to the cabin—she could see Jake ahead of her, almost at the door, and she could see Patti coming out. Alice stopped and stepped to one side, slightly behind a large maple.

She watched Jake and Patti approach each other, touch and merge. She watched their long embrace, and she wondered why *she* wasn't ever embraced like that. It left her feeling empty, as if something had been stolen from her. And although she knew that what she witnessed wasn't perfect, still, she wanted it for her own. She wanted it back.

She stood watching for a long time, even after they went inside. Occasional laughter drifted through the open door. She wondered what it must be like for them when they made love—how gentle they were, who did the touching, who got touched, if they ever truly connected.

As Alice listened to the sound of her wind chimes increasing, she wondered if the chimes were quiet at her own house, and she wanted them to be ringing there. She wanted them to be ringing at Mona's house, and even at Liza's; she wanted the sound of her chimes to ring up and down the valley.

And she wanted the wind to increase to a gale, melody to cacophony, blowing all the other sounds away, whispers and laughter and self-serving definitions of love. She wanted to fill the whole valley with the clamor of wind chimes, until everyone, everywhere, would have to stop, and listen.

CHAPTER **9**

Birth

Matt

At midnight she shakes me awake, fingernails deep in
my flesh. Sharp pain, shattered dreams, Alice Bourne.
"They're starting already," she says.
    "Right," I answer, "Okay. Let's go." I find her wrists.
"Let go." For a moment I sit next to her, rubbing my eyes,
rubbing my shoulders. "I'll go down and start the truck. Get
your things." I kiss her forehead. "I'll be back to give you a
hand." Downstairs I pull on heavy clothes in a rush, but
outside it's hopeless—snow continues to fall as thickly as I've
ever seen it, and the night is black as only a starless, moonless
night in the deep country can be. The new snow is already well
over my knees as I forge down the hill looking for the footbridge with the beam of the flashlight. When I get to the road it
hasn't been plowed, not even once since the storm began, and
my truck is just a small drift in the snowy landscape. I turn
around and climb back to the house.
    Alice is more than a week early, but I think I knew
before her contractions began that she'd give birth with this
storm. Snow had started falling yesterday morning; by sunset
the accumulation was already the greatest we'd seen all winter.
And the radio called for the storm to continue at least for
another day and night.
    Inside Alice is pulling my insulated overalls over her
swollen belly. "We can't do it," I say. "The plow hasn't come
through yet." She sucks in a deep breath and puts her hands on
her hips. "There's no chance, not even with four-wheel-drive.
We'll just get stuck in the middle of the night somewhere.
Without any help." Alice nods, and I can tell she is thinking
that's already happened.

When I pick up the telephone the line is dead. That's what you get from doing things half-assed. We live too far away for power, half a mile up the road from Liza's place, where the poles stop. At first I liked the isolation, but two months ago I got a spool of used cable from a friend who worked at the telephone company and I laid wire across the forest floor to Liza's house. But now everything is reduced to this house and this storm.

I'm not ready for this. I have three books, I've been to eight classes, but still, I don't know anything about childbirth. I open the first book to the section on contractions. Mostly it talks about calling the doctor, getting to the hospital, what to bring. The Merck Manual isn't any better—it's way too concise, assumes far too much. The third book is Patti's homebirth manual. I hadn't looked at it much before—homebirth wasn't something I wanted to put Alice through.

Patti is our second coach. She's been here every day to check on Alice, even yesterday, before the roads got too bad. She'd planned to be present in the delivery room. "Don't worry," I've heard her say. "It's not so bad. I've just been through it; I know. Piece of cake."

"Piece of cake?" Alice once asked incredulously.

"Well," Patti explained, "you forget the pain later."

Now Alice paces around the great room. She wants the fire built up in the stove, wants the futon brought down from the loft, wants water heated for a shower. I do all of these things. I heat a second tank of water; Alice takes another shower, later a third. After several hours her contractions slacken, and she lies down on the futon where I've moved it into the corner. She's still naked from her last shower and she pulls the sheet and blanket up to her neck. Soon she dozes off.

I sit on the edge of the futon next to her and start reading Patti's book. Alice stirs in her sleep, pushing her body around, trying to get comfortable, trying to find a place where her belly might fit, but there isn't any. She throws off her covers and lies on her back, knees bent, feet flat, legs apart.

The room is very warm; I've stripped down to my T-shirt. I reach over and pull just the sheet up to her shoulders. And it's like I've dropped a snake on her—she shouts in her sleep, grabs the sheet and flings it off, begins thrashing around so violently I'm afraid she'll hurt herself. The skin over her belly is stretched so tight it could burst with a touch. I reach over, try to restrain her, but she pushes me away, swearing, calling out, "Louis," and then moaning, "No."

I've learned not to disturb those dreams. I woke her once, before I knew better, and she emerged like an animal, all teeth and fangs, snarling. She nearly took out my eye, snapping and spitting, her hands like claws. She gouged my cheek so deeply it bled before I could I grab her wrists, force her backwards down onto the bed and hold her there. Then I didn't know what to do—I was afraid to let go. But quickly another change came over her, and she abruptly stopped struggling. She'd been so incredibly strong; suddenly her body went completely limp. A weird smile like a leer distorted her face. I'm convinced she was neither awake nor asleep. She spread her legs apart. "Take me then," she said, hissing. Then she started to laugh, a loud hysterical sound, and I dropped one of her wrists and slapped her twice. She was stunned for a minute, staring. "Louis?" she asked, and then "Matt?" and then she asked angrily, "Why did you hit me, Matt?"

"You were having a nightmare," I said. "Or something." But she denied it later, or didn't remember, and afterwards she wouldn't make love with me for almost two weeks.

Louis. I'd been piecing his history together ever since I first met Alice. There was a flaw in Alice Bourne, a fracture so deep and old it went beyond her childhood. I'm not perfect either—I have my own ghosts. But they're nothing like hers, nothing like her father, her mother, her uncle. Louis.

That first time was just the beginning. Louis returned a few weeks later, in the middle part of a broad sunny afternoon, a time I'd learned was most likely to allow lovemaking. I was flat on my back and Alice was astride me, about to climax, her eyes hooded the way they always got, her head back and her mouth open just a little. She was rhythmically moaning— *oou, oou, oou*—her full lower lip caught on her even teeth, her whole face compressing tension, her body arching like a bow. But when she climaxed she closed her eyes, and the sound of her ecstasy became his name—*Louis, Louis, Louis.* I couldn't stand it; I rolled out from under her. I dressed in silence and left the house. Outside it was a beautiful sun-filled afternoon, but there was nowhere to go. No place anywhere.

Alice Bourne. We have been married less than a year, distanced by ghosts, distanced by pregnancy. Now we are having a child together. I reach out and touch her, but not too hard—I'm careful not to wake her. Alice Bourne. The only way I can touch her now is when she's asleep. And then only if I'm so gentle that she cannot feel me.

Now we are having a child. That may save us, I think—save her, save me. Alice as mother, a primal thing, powerful enough to displace the ghosts in her life. And maybe there'd be room for me in it then, someplace normal, someplace useful, someplace that mattered. Father, protector, parent, provider.

Because I don't fit as a husband anymore. I don't fit as a lover. Already we've used up that part of our marriage. In her eyes I have become Louis now. And making love with Alice Bourne is something to talk about in the past tense.

Pregnancy consumes desire. The few times we tried usual lovemaking Alice complained of the hurt, but when we tried different positions they were each a disaster. The last time we made love was months ago; Alice became hysterical when she couldn't see my face, convinced I was Louis. Even after I turned her in my arms she couldn't tell who I was; she just continued screaming, kicking, clawing; she began shouting for her dog. And then Lancelot, scrabbling around at the foot of the steep loft stairs, furious and frustrated, Lancelot was suddenly in our midst, growling, snarling, lunging for me, lunging for Louis. Louis and Lancelot. All in a second.

I beat them both down.

Often it seems so hopeless. But still, there are times even now, lying in bed in that vague pleasant space between sleep and wakefulness, when it feels as if all of my life has been simply a pathway to get to the place where I am: next to Alice Bourne.

Alice Bourne. Now a child. Now a mother. Now she can leave her own childhood behind her.

Finally she becomes still. I draw the sheet up to her shoulders and she leaves it there. I put my hand on her forehead—it's cool, almost clammy. I gather towels, sheets. I put more wood in the stove, I heat more water. Alice dozes in and out of restfulness, calling on her mother, calling on Louis. I go outside and check the storm—it's snowing more than ever. It's about three in the morning. Inside, I read about dilation in Patti's book.

I get a flashlight, pull down the sheet gently. Alice doesn't wake up. She still lies on her back, her legs spread and I try to determine how much she's dilated, but it's impossible to see anything, and I don't want to probe around between her legs when she's asleep. I wish there were someone to help. I try the telephone again, but it's still dead. I sit by Alice's side, reading the same pages over and over.

I'm not sure Alice ever really wanted to have a child. She's been depressed about it for nine months. I know she never planned to get pregnant; on the other hand we have never discussed abortion. But there is a lot we never talk about. Alice talks to Patti, though, and Patti talks to me.

Alice was so convinced she was going to have a girl we'd only considered one name. But she was afraid there would be something wrong with her daughter. Her premonition was constant. She was always asking Patti what her own pregnancy had felt like. "I don't want to do this," she'd end up saying. "I don't want this child."

At dawn Alice wakes up screaming. The contractions have started for real. I arrange pillows around her, bend over her face, start to coach her with breathing. She's in a lot of pain, and having trouble managing it.

All morning long her contractions become increasingly frequent and severe. By ten o'clock they are only about three minutes apart; I'm timing them with my watch now. Each one lasts more than a minute, although it seems much longer than that. Alice leans back against my chest; I've taken her spot on the futon, my back against the pillows against the wall. We are breathing together through the worst of the pain, panting together like dogs, slick with sweat. The books have dropped to the floor. Outside, snow falls heavily.

Every half hour or so I push my ear against her belly and count the baby's heartbeats, although I'm not sure what good it does. There's no one to call if they're too fast or slow. But the books say to do it. Her belly is as hard as a drum head.

And the books say to do vaginal exams, so I probe around with my fingers now, trying to determine what progress the head has made in descending, how much Alice has dilated. It's not easy. Alice is in no mood to cooperate. I've measured the diameter of my index finger—it's two centimeters. The opening of her cervix seems to be at least three times that. My fingers have been here many times before, but nothing feels familiar.

Just before noon her waters break, a rush of clear liquid that startles us both. Alice rolls to one side and I change the bedding, prop her back up against pillows. "It's okay," I tell her. "Patti's book says there's two quarts of amniotic fluid." She screams and we breathe.

Soon after that she begins to bleed and for the first time I feel truly frightened. I sponge her clean, probe around. Four fingers would fit in the opening of her cervix now. We breathe through a contraction. I listen to the baby's heartbeat, hold her hand, breathe through another contraction, read through the books. "I don't think it's bright red," I tell her. She screams and we breathe. "I don't think it's fresh blood coming from your vagina."

"Shut up, Matt," she says, then screams again. Her contractions now seem to last as long as the intervals in between. I time them again with my watch. Actually they're lasting longer. And each time a little more water and blood leaks out of Alice. I sponge her clean, check the book. "I need to push now," she says.

"You can't," I say. "It's still too early. Breathe with me." Each contraction catches her by surprise, leaves her gasping. We breathe. Her contractions seem back-to-back for a long time, then they slacken for a moment. I listen to her belly, probe around inside her. Her cervix is so wide I could pass my hand through it.

"She's killing me, Matt." I hold her hands. "Oh my god my god my back," she screams and we start to breathe. Alice starts to tremble, then she is sweating profusely. "Something's wrong," she says. I listen to her belly.

"It's okay. Breathe."

"I'm cold, Matt," she says. "Where's Patti?"

I pull a blanket around us. "She'll be here," I say.

And then she is—the door opens and closes and Patti is inside. "You made it," I say, turning around. "The roads are open." But I wonder if it's too late now to attempt the drive, and what the conditions are. I see us in a ditch. "What are the roads like?"

"There aren't any. I skied over," Patti says, stripping off her hat and gloves and coat by the doorway. Alice vomits suddenly over the two of us, then screams again. I clean us up and Patti helps.

"Patti, where *were* you?" Alice demands. "I'm so hot now." And then she is interrupted by another contraction. "Oh god it hurts so much so much oh fuck," she says.

"Breathe with me," Patti says.

"I can't," says Alice, and she screams again. Then she lies back panting.

"How dilated is she?" Patti asks me, washing her hands at the sink.

"Almost there."

Patti probes between Alice's legs during her next contraction. "You're doing just great, Alice," she says. "I can feel your baby's head. You can start pushing now."

"I can't," she says. "It's too late."

Patti takes my place, has me get towels and warm water and washcloths. Behind me I can hear her urging Alice to push. When I return Patti folds warm wet compresses and applies them between Alice's legs. Alice lies moaning, swearing between contractions. "Push," she says to Alice. "Bear down each time. You're doing great."

"It's not working," Alice says. She looks worried. I glance at Patti.

"She's okay, Matt. It's normal. Boil some water. We need to sterilize some scissors. Your sharpest ones." I nod. "And shoelaces. Three of them. White ones." I nod again. "Thirty minutes. A rolling boil."

"Okay," I say. I touch her shoulder. "I'm glad you're here, Patti."

She smiles, Alice groans. "Push, Alice," Patti says. "Bear down each time now. You're doing great."

"I don't want this," Alice says. "I don't want to do this." I take her hands. "Leave me alone, Matt. Leave me alone." Then she cries out, swearing. Patti motions with her head and I release Alice's hands. I put a pan of water on the iron Glenwood; I stoke it with wood. I go after the things Patti needs.

When I return Patti is listening to Alice's belly. "You're still doing fine," she says. Alice seems to be resting longer between contractions now. "Look, Matt," Patti says, and I can see the baby's head pushing at the outer lips of Alice's vagina, then it disappears within. I watch in fascination. With Alice's next contraction it appears again, then recedes as she relaxes. "Get a mirror," Patti says. "And some olive oil." She shows me how to massage Alice's perineum. Patti has another list of things we need—a rubber syringe, a large unbreakable bowl, more warm water and towels, sanitary napkins, receiving blankets. I collect everything except the syringe. All I can find is the small poultry baster which I drop into the boiling water on the Glenwood. I return with everything else, and then sit beside Alice again, holding her hand.

It takes another hour for the head to crown, but after that everything happens quickly. Patti can't get Alice to stop pushing now. She places one hand over the top of the baby's head and slips her other just slightly under Alice's vagina. "Coach her, Matt," she says impatiently.

I lean over Alice's face. "Don't push anymore," I say. "You're almost there. You're great. Breathe with me." With her next contraction I breathe light rapid relaxed breaths. Alice is with me for just a moment, then she clenches her teeth, closes her eyes, pushes as hard as she can.

"Get out of my face," she gasps. "Stop telling me how to breathe." Then she screams as her tissues tear. Our baby's head appears between her legs. Slate blue. Patti runs her hand around the child's neck. Alice pushes again and again, scream-ing, one shoulder comes, then the other, then our child is born. Patti places him on Alice's belly, covers him with a receiving blanket.

"No," Alice moans, and I grab the baby as Alice rolls onto her side. Blood is leaking out between her legs. Bright red. Fresh from her vagina.

"Support his head," Patti says, and I realize our child is a boy, short stubby penis undeniable, and I wonder how Alice could have been so thoroughly wrong, so adamant about naming the child Alice Bourne. He meets my eyes for an instant and his eyes are deep blue, blue as cobalt, and it's like looking into a night sky, infinitely deep and drawingly beauti-ful. "Matt," Patti says, "Come on." And I hold my son's head so she can use the baster to suck mucus out of his nose and mouth and throat. He yells, but starts to breathe; he starts to turn pink before my eyes. Patti has me double tie the cord and cut it, then she reaches down, pulls the slack cord out of Alice,

and makes a third tie near her vagina. She examines the tears
for a moment. I hold our baby against my chest, rubbing him
through the blanket. He continues yelling and I can't make him
stop. Mostly I'm worried about Alice, though.

Patti makes her squat over a bowl while she lightly
massages Alice's stomach and stimulates her nipples until the
placenta is expelled in a gush of blood. Only after she picks it
up and examines it carefully does she pack several sanitary
napkins between Alice's legs and let her lie down again.

She takes my son from me and hands him to Alice.
"He needs to nurse now," she tells her.

"No," Alice moans. She folds her arms across her
chest. "It's a boy," she whispers, her voice full of astonish-
ment, tinged with disgust. She doesn't take him. She looks
like she's going to die.

"Give her a minute," Patti says, passing the baby back
to me. Then she pushes her long dark hair out of her eyes,
reaches down and unbuttons her shirt. She unclasps her
brassiere; her breasts are still heavy and swollen with milk from
nursing Brittany. She reaches out for our son.

Alice watches, her eyes hardening. She draws in
breath with a steady sucking hiss. "He's mine," she says.
"Pass him over." She leans forward abruptly and roughly takes
him, grunting, pulling him down toward her own breasts. He
nuzzles blindly, ineffectually, and Alice takes her nipple herself
and impatiently slides it into his mouth. He clamps down hard
and her eyes suddenly widen; then instinct takes over, nursing
irresistible, primordial. Alice leans back against the pillows;
her eyes gradually close, and gradually her face changes—
slowly it's suffused with peace, and slowly she smiles. She
looks like a madonna. I reach over and gently touch her
shoulder, but her eyes flutter open, and she pushes my hand
away.

Patti refastens her clothes. She washes between
Alice's legs, looking carefully, then repacks Alice with new
napkins. "You need to boil needles now, and heavy thread.

She's going to need stitches." I look at Alice and shake my head. I feel so weary. She and the baby are already starting to doze, sleep coming thick and heavy over them both. Patti puts her hand on my shoulder. "You should take a nap, too. We can't do anything for half an hour."

"I'll never wake up."

"Yes, you will."

I sit down in the rocker and instantly fall asleep. Almost immediately Patti is calling my name. Alice is shouting, our son is squalling, Patti is sitting astride one of Alice's legs, unable to hold the other still. A needle glints silver in her free hand. "Hold her, Matt," she says without turning around. I try to calm Alice, but Alice is furious, bracing herself with her hands and trying to squirm out from under Patti, twisting her body from side to side. "Just hold her, Matt. Just get it done," Patti says, and I lean sideways across Alice's belly, my back to her face. Alice swears at us both, pounding my back with her clenched fists. Patti's face is scratched and bleeding, and she looks as grim and angry as I've ever seen her.

I'm careful not to put any weight on Alice's stomach, but I push her knees down firmly and I force her legs apart. Behind me I hear her hissing. I'm afraid to turn around. Patti puts in five stitches, as quickly and neatly as if she were sewing buttons on a shirt. In about a minute she's finished; she gets up and goes to the sink to wash. I turn to Alice then, but her different faces are all merging together, coalescing into something new: she is seething, hissing, absolutely unapproachable.

I join Patti at the sink. "Now what?" I ask.

"*Now* what? Now it's time for me to go home, Matt." I glance back at Alice, then at Patti. She pushes her hair back from her face. "I thought I could let you sleep." She turns away from me and looks out the window. I'm too tired to understand. "She's *your* wife, Matt," Patti explains. "I'm all done here." Outside it's still snowing heavily.

CHAPTER 10

Loving

Alice

At the altar set in chimney stone, Mona lights candles, ritual and red. Her body curves forward, a small flame flickering in her hands. When she straightens, she presses her fingertips together, a temple at her chest. I watch her light the incense next, slowly wave the glowing wand, her beauty graceful, sinuous as the wistful smoke suspended now in still air, like memory, filling the room with scent. Mona begins to chant the heart sutra. I listen to my own heart.

People talk about loving all the time. Some kind of existential union. Heart and soul, body and spirit. A perfect fusion of matching halves. But me?

I am just flesh.

I wake in the morning to Matt behind me, not even a name. Mindless, faceless, too dull for rape. I'm not *me* anymore; that's what I hate so much. Just flesh—warm, soft, moist meat.

Whisper your dreams, Matthew. I'm taking my body back.

Mona's voice breaks up my thoughts: "Sit straighter, *mon amie.*" Mona my teacher, my friend, my mentor Mona. "Imagine the silver thread, pulling you up." Mona the meditation queen—thick red hair, breasts soft and arrogant and arching so far forward when she sits meditating that even I want to pillow my head on them, sleep there forever. I look into her eyes often enough, but I can never tell what color they are—they change; they take on available light.

Matt and I aren't lovers anymore. I don't want to be his wife anymore, either. I'm a mother now, and that's enough.

Whisper your dreams. The circle is closing: there's no more room, and no way inside.

"Straighter, *mon amie*." Mona puts a hand on my stomach, a hand low on my back. "And no thinking." She slides her hands slowly up and away, brushing my shoulder blades, my breasts, my nipples.

How can one *not* think? Thoughts swirl endlessly, relentlessly—films unreeling in my head. My marriage with Matt, failing from the moment it began. Always the ghosts between us. Uncle Louis. The dark woman. The arc from the hollow to the homestead a gray rainbow.

I dream. That last night in the hollow, first night with Matt. I thought I'd lost them forever, those ghosts, so sure I'd left them behind, washed out of Bourne Hollow in the flood. Washed out in that incredible loving with Matt. The only time when it was simple and pure, when there was just me, Alice, the child, finally free. But they came back. Louis and the dark woman.

In the beginning she was a sacrifice, a savior. When I was twelve, my body first changing, my uncle would come to me. I'd smile at him and then look down, the way I'd seen women do with men. The first night he came into my room I thought it would be sweet. In the stories it was always sweet. I was Alice Bourne, leaping to womanhood, and I thought no one could stop me. I was taking my mother's place. But Louis stopped me, stiff and huge and hurting. It wasn't sweet at all.

Then I discovered the cave. I lined it with moss and fern. And when Uncle Louis came into my room the next night the little girl wriggled down into it, where only she could fit. And the dark woman came out, stood guard at the entrance. The dark woman met Louis. And she enjoyed it.

Louis would climax, holding my body, calling my name. "Alice, Alice, Alice" still reverberates through time, words lost and seeking. But I was never to be found; only the dark woman was there to be found. She caught the name as though it belonged to her; she wore it like her own.

Sometimes Louis would offer me whiskey and the dark woman would take it and I couldn't stop her and she would drink it down, and drive the child Alice down, down, and Louis would be grinning, waiting for her, for me.

Always his face I saw as I was driven down. His face waiting and waiting, grinning. The dark woman drinking, unquenchable thirst for everything. Alice peering out of the cave. Waking in the morning sick, dark woman wanting everything, sick, more of everything.

"No thinking, *mon amie*. Empty your mind of thought."

I study Mona's floor; the wide chestnut boards have become as familiar as the world, as constant as friends should be. Finely smoothed and thick with several coats of glossy varnish, knot holes and defects filled with reddish resin, red warmth down in the wood, deeply glowing, beginning of space.

The name Alice Bourne has always been in our family. My mother had that name, my grandmother, her mother before her. Mothers and daughters. Women of the hollow.

When I was young, my name was just Alice.

"Alice," Louis would say, "Alice." But after the first night the young girl was gone; the person who met Louis was a grown woman, generations old, as old as the names in the graveyards, the ruined cellar holes, the hills themselves, Alice Bourne.

So who did Matthew get to meet? He met us both, in quick succession. For one shining instant he met Alice, loved Alice, and Alice loved him. Thunder and lightning. Then the dark woman.

"No thinking, *ma cherie*."

Mona is teaching me meditation. Teaching me patience. Mindfulness and awareness. Two wings of a bird. Mona from Quebec Province, the Eastern Townships. *Where I come from they all drive old cars and live in trailers.* When she smiles her teeth are different colors, and the scar across her cheek becomes narrow and thin.

I sit in her living room. She has foam inserts in the windows now and her house is snug, sounder than any house I've ever known. One can hear the wind outside as it smashes into the walls, but there is no feeling of it within. Cherry trimmed sheetrock among the posts and beams, everything solid and safe. Candles burn on the house altar, incense fills the room.

Mona is teaching me the practice, teaching me to dismiss thought. But all I can do is think. I sit on the red and yellow cushion, my back straight, the silver thread, legs crossed, hands folded. Focus on my breathing. Red and yellow cushion. Gomden. Zabuton. Try not to think.

But I am all thought, nothing but thought. I think about Matt and I think about Mona. I've seen them approach each other, circling like dancers, dancing like fighters. Soaring like hawks, searching for prey. Who is the prey? Vultures cruising carrion.

Mindfulness and awareness. Two wings of a bird. Bird in flight. I will fly.

The sound of the night wind outside. Clocks ticking. Fire in the wood stove softly snapping. The winter snow.

Thinking and thinking and thinking.

I think about Matt and I think about loving. What do I know about loving? Most of my life I've been in a cave, a cave in the hollow, a child alone.

There is in the Caribbean a plant whose leaves curl up when it's touched. I was like that. Louis touching me. Night after night after night. That was love for me: curling up, withdrawing into the cave. Uncle Louis at the door. The dark woman at the door. Keeping him out, keeping me in. Body-guard to prison guard.

Matt was the breakout. I'd tried to break out before. Boys in college who knew so much less than I did. Matt set me free. That night in the flood I was free. Free and for once completely empowered. I could call everything down, and I did: thunder and lightning, hail and snow, the old mill dam at

Bourne Pond, the mountain itself. Scour the hollow, the ghost of my mother, Louis, the trailer we shared. Wash away everything, the river in flood. I was the one. I did that.

Also, I was in love. Awakening to Matt's hands and kisses and sex as joy. But it didn't last. Nothing lasts.

Matt was no match for Louis. Sometimes in the dark, Matt's hand on my breast, I would feel Louis there; my body would tense and reject him. I would hear Louis hiss in the night, the way a snake would laugh. And Matt could never understand.

I was no match for the dark woman. The problem with Louis was that some part of me liked it. While part of me curled up, part of me came out. I would become my mother, her mother, her mother before her. Alice Bourne. The dark woman.

"Alice, Alice, *ma cherie*. They're just thoughts. They're not real. Let them go."

Matt liked to wake in the night, lick me until I was moist and slide into me while I was still half asleep. And I would come apart in my sleep, already broken by dreams. Wake up with Alice gone, the small cave, the dark woman outside. Wake up to Matt without or Louis within—I could not tell, just the rhythmic pushing, pushing. It was like losing a fight.

The dark woman would wake and turn to Matt as if he were Louis, loving and hating him, calling him back, calling him Louis by name. And Matt would say, "But that's all over; that's all over now."

But it wasn't over at all. And the more I tried to tell Matt that Louis still existed, the more distant Matt became. The more like Louis he became.

"Breathe deep, *ma cherie*. From here." Mona's hands low on my belly, over my uterus; I think of Christopher. Mona's hands gently pressing. "That's better, yes. That's better." Mona's hands lingering.

Mona teach me about loving.

I don't think the dark woman knew anything about loving. It was Alice who married. Alice who made love that night in the flood. When I first went to Matt's house I knew exactly where I was going. In a world of darkness there was one light, a beacon. A world of shades, and Matt's light.

Matt. A fetus came between us. Said like that, it sounds like I aborted our child, but that isn't true, of course. The truth is that he was much more than a physical thing, expanding belly and hormones all changing. He was distance between us. He was growing in my head and in my heart.

Still, when he was born he wasn't mine. He wasn't even a girl.

Unlike some women, I *never* forget pain. And bearing Christopher was one long endless scream. Hours and hours on that thin blue futon, lumpy pillows, my legs spread apart, screaming. Patti and Matt wouldn't leave me alone, their faces huge in mine, chanting: *push, push, push.* But I couldn't push; I couldn't breathe. I was screaming—screaming and screaming until at last that whole room contracted and the child was expelled.

Now there is Christopher, a suckling babe, lying against my chest, my nipple filling his mouth, small round lips surrounding me. Where there used to be Matt. And before him Louis. I'll never be free.

I don't think the dark woman was ever meant to be a mother. Not once. Not ever. Not in any of the generations.

An hour into the practice I have to urinate. The expanding need accomplishes what meditation cannot, and for a long time I sit without thinking, feeling only my bladder distending. Finally I go outside.

The outhouse behind Mona's cabin is as fine a room as any I've ever seen, spacious and light, yellow pine and cherry trim and oval window. Through the window the moon is full behind the falling snow; a broad hazy ring surrounds it. The wind has stopped. Snow drifts down in huge quiet flakes, soft and silent as feathers.

Back inside Mona's cabin, sitting on the red and yellow cushion again, I think of feathers, snow, the snow owl behind the house I built with Matt. I grow tired, and finally I drift away, drop down, snowy owl, silently gliding, feathery wings, downy tufts, softly slipping through quiet air, cirrus clouds wispy, feathery, high and free and scudding, and I am drifting, finally, drifting into the meditative space, slipping away, falling into the meditative space—eyes closed, mouth open ever so slightly.

I feel Mona's breath, a whisper. I am surprised how natural her kiss feels. Brushing my lips her tongue is soft and moist, quick against my front teeth—my mouth opens a little wider and Mona is within. It is her taste that is so nice. And the movement, the slow quickness. And the feel of her, hard softness exploring and probing and caressing. Mona within me. I open my mouth wider still and kiss her back. I don't open my eyes though, until after she draws away. She sits apart on her own cushion, her back absolutely straight, looking directly ahead. No sign. Perhaps she thinks I imagined everything. I study her face. Her eyes slowly close.

Mona sits next to me, body arched, breasts proud. I return to my breathing. I don't really want to learn meditation. What good is that? I want to learn about loving. There is no hope anymore, just loneliness, gray bondage.

After the closing chant Mona extinguishes the candles. The room grows small, thick with the waxy smoke I always associate with churches. I stretch my shoulders and arch my back, my legs stiff, still cross-legged on the red and yellow cushion. Slowly private spaces merge into a common one. The flowers on the altar become intensely bright, yellow and blue. I can smell Mona's body near me, pungent, spicy. She stands up, helps me to my feet. She puts her arms around me and it feels so natural I hug her back and we stand like that for a long moment, pressed together, our bodies merging. Mona moves her hands up and down my back, space dissolving, bodies coalescing, and then she kisses me again; her lips seal over mine. Her hand on the back of my neck presses my face to hers and her other hand slides around my side under my shirt sudden and cold and cupping my breast. I break the spell, break the embrace, I step away.

I can hear them hissing, Louis and the dark woman. Greedy, grasping, looking for something new. But I banish the dark woman. And Louis I never acknowledge at all.

My eyes fasten on Mona's and even as I draw away I am drawn in; her eyes become larger and deeper and I am falling into them. Mona's house is lit with dull silver light; her eyes flash and glint as she talks. Her voice is full and soft, and she touches my body as she speaks, points for emphasis, points to ground herself, as if she is trying to solidify the ideas she's forming. Love as trust. The safety of women. Their yielding softness.

And even though I think I might keep those ghosts at bay, and even though Mona's kisses are sweet, her body soft and warm and beautiful embrace, still I stand apart. I want simple love, the love that everyone else has just granted to them, that they assume as their right. I deserve that, too.

I want hard arms and firm legs, muscled power to wrap around me. I want to be contained, sustained, enveloped and held, surrounded by strength. I want to find my *other* half—I don't want to duplicate this one.

I try to listen to the snow fall outside. Try to listen to this woman who has never had a child, but always had men. Mona and men—she doesn't need men; men need her. Mona living in the snowy winter, quiet in her house alone.

I need to learn about loving, simple loving. I am so tired of being alone. Words go through my head—my own heart sutra—birth and death, women and men, Mona and Matt, Louis and the dark woman. There are limits to the loving I can give. I am a mother now, I am *my* mother now. The circle is closing, and I am alone within it, dancing without a partner, the dark woman waiting.

Mona teach me about loving, simple loving.
Teach me about men.

Chapter 11

Transformations

Patti

It's really getting crowded now. The pullets are only a month old, but they outgrew their crate behind the cookstove weeks ago. They're not cute at all anymore, and they're beginning to smell. Finally this morning I got Jake to start the carpentry in the chickenhouse.

I've raised them on chick starter, and they've grown fast. Corn meal mash and warm water—it looks just like breakfast cereal, yellow and grainy, warm and wet. *Corn meal mush,* Jake calls it, and I can't feed him grits or cream of wheat or even oatmeal for breakfast anymore. He says it's bad enough having the chickens live in his kitchen; he's not going to share their diet, too. Chickens, Christ. They were *his* idea in the first place. When I was a kid we used to raise horses, Tennessee Walkers.

Jake says it's finally going to warm up today. I say it's about time. It's June now and I'm still running this wood stove every single morning, chucking white oak and rock maple down into the narrow firebox, coals glowing in there red and orange, just waiting, barely contained, like passion—one instant to flare up, break out, consume everything. I clank the iron lids back into place. The stove smokes a little and I adjust the chimney damper.

It would be summer at home by now. Up here it's supposed to be spring. And I'm supposed to be making a fancy apple crisp for Sunday breakfast. Matt and Alice are coming over for a sauna. Mona was supposed to come, too, but yesterday she told me she'd seen enough of Alice for awhile. I don't have the energy to deal with them anymore. I'm tired,

and I just want to rest. Last night I couldn't sleep at all—
thunder kept crashing me awake, rolling blasts that shook this
house right down to its foundations, over and over and over
again. It felt like lightning was right in the dooryard, right in
the bedroom, right in the bed itself. Set this whole place on
fire, blow everything apart. Jake slept through the entire night
as if it were normal. But things have been strange for a while
now. Maybe the climate's changing; I don't know. Thunder-
storms up here are never as intense as the one last night, and
they never come before July. That's when my due date is.

The solid thunking of hammer on wood echoes across
the yard, rhythmic and steady. Jake is good at building things.
He built this little cabin for himself, then the sugarhouse. After
we got married he put up the sauna and the chickenhouse,
identical versions of each other. Now with children coming
faster than you can count he's been building the house addition.
Nursing mothers can't get pregnant. Yeah, right.

Usually I do my share around here. Usually I'm full of
energy. But all this June I've been as slow as the spring. It's
starting to feel like I've been pregnant forever. Up until
recently I didn't mind it much—I just felt heavy and content,
like one of Mona's Buddhas. It's hard to describe—I felt at
peace with myself. Expansive. A child at my breast, a child in
my belly. Like I'd transcended my own self, like my physical
body had become a whole family, and even Jake was a part of
me, too. Mona's been trying to teach Alice meditation, transcendence. Mona should try having babies instead. Teach
Alice what *that* can be like. I worry about Alice.

It was Jake's idea to take a sauna today. I can't do that,
eight months pregnant. Besides, that's a winter thing to do. I
want to transplant tomato seedlings, put in corn, start squash
and pumpkins.

Brittany is complaining in her playpen and the chicks
are noisy in their box. *This kitchen used to smell so nice.* I'm
getting cabin fever. I slice up apples and sprinkle on the
topping, slide the pan into the oven and adjust the stove

dampers. I give Brittany her pacifier and wander into the house addition Jake has been working on for the last year and a half now.

We need this extra space. Houses are like marriages—structures to contain things; they take forever to get right. People and passion and history. Always changing their form. They take a lot of work to keep up. And they sure can come down in a hurry. Wood stoves and fire. Thunder and lightning.

I think what's most important is the ability to create things. Head and heart and hands. I'm as good as Jake when it comes to creating things. But it takes energy to do that, energy that gets taken from you forever, becomes bound up in the thing itself like a coiled spring. As if built into the thing is the need to come undone, the need to release all of that folded force. Alice tried to convince me once that love was like that, universal force all bound up and ready to explode, energy and destruction. Thunder and lightning. Alice and Matt. Coming together, coming apart.

Now she comes with Christopher, six months old. She's playing the wind chimes by the kitchen door, but he's not paying any attention. She says Matt had to stay home to work on Christopher's room, but I can tell they've been fighting again. Jake comes in, and we all have breakfast together, talking about chickens mostly. But the subject we're skirting is whether Jake and Alice will take a sauna by themselves.

Jake helps himself to a third piece of apple crisp. "The wall's all studded up," he says. "I framed the door and hung it, too. All it needs now is the wire mesh stapled."

"Great," I say. "You could finish this morning."

"Nope," he says. "I'm done with chicken condos. Sunday is my day off."

"They really are starting to smell, Jake," I point out.

Alice wrinkles her nose. "They used to be so adorable," she says.

"They get uglier every day," Jake laughs. "That's how chickens grow."

They *are* ugly now, but I remember when they were a day old, airy fluff, yellow as their starter mash. You could hold one in the palm of your hand. Brittany helped me name them and their names are a secret only we understand. There are eleven of them now; one died a few days after they arrived. Brittany hugged her too hard I think; you've got to control your feelings.

"They think Patti's their mother," Jake says. "They follow her around like ducklings." And it's true they've bonded to me. They recognize my voice and I say they even recognize their names, but Jake says that's impossible, they're only chickens, the dumbest animals there are. He says their brains aren't even big enough to allow them smooth move-ment—they just ratchet around, clicking their heads sideways to look at you with those single beady chicken eyes. I'll be glad to move them out of here. They need to have their own space in the chickenhouse, though, otherwise the older chick-ens will kill them.

After breakfast Alice draws me aside, and she's polite enough to ask if it's okay for her to go off and take a sauna with my husband. "I guess," I say, although I don't know about Alice anymore.

"Can you watch Christopher for me?"

"Yeah, of course."

Jake is right about the day—finally it is beginning to warm up outdoors—so before they leave I have him move the playpen under the maple for Brittany and Christopher. I play with them for a while, then go into the chickenhouse to finish what Jake has started. But I don't have the energy to swing a hammer anymore. I put it down and gaze out the chickenhouse window. Last night's storm blew down most of the lilac petals; they cover the ground under the bushes like snow. The grass sparkles in the sun; everything is wet and fresh and smells like promise. Brittany and Christopher doze peacefully under the maple.

I don't know about Matt and Alice. People should be happy with what they've got. They've got a beautiful child,

and they could work on their marriage. I like Matt better the
more I know him, but ever since Christopher's birth I've started
to like Alice less. First she wants her child, then she doesn't
want her child, then she wants her child again and now she
wants him so much that there's no room for anything else.
Except that she's still complaining because her son isn't a girl.
Incredible.

Now she won't let anyone even touch Christopher.
Not me, not Mona, not Jake. Not even Matt. Except when it's
convenient for her, like today, so she can take a sauna with my
husband.

I turn back to my work and cut a section of chicken
wire with Jake's heavy blue tin snips. Putting up this wall
would have been a piece of cake three years ago. All I have to
do is snip out the chicken wire and tack it with small fencing
staples. I pick up my hammer again, but I'm too pregnant to do
this. My belly gets in the way; my child is kicking. Mostly I
can't stop thinking about Alice with Jake. I don't like suspicion—it takes on a life of its own too quickly—so I decide to
take the children and walk over to the sauna. But as soon as I
step outside I can smell the smoke, and even though there's not
much here, just wisps in the wind, I know immediately that it's
more than just chimney smoke. Brittany's awake now; she sees
me and gurgles, gripping her pink plastic hammer with both
hands, sucking the handle. I leave her with Christopher and
hurry to the sauna house. It's a long way from the cabin to the
road, past the sugarhouse to the sauna, and I can't move very
fast. Everything is so green and dense and slow.

I can hear the fire roaring before I can see it, and
suddenly I'm overwhelmed with guilt, of all things. By the
time I reach the clearing the whole building is wrapped in
flames, and I can't even get near it. Flames tear up the walls,
spread thirty feet into the air—the whole front façade is a sheet
of fire. The door is still closed and Jake and Alice aren't
anywhere in sight. I shout their names until I am hoarse. I
keep trying to get close; I keep getting driven back. There is a

brook by the sauna but no way to move water. It seems unbelievable that they could be trapped inside, but I don't know. There is just the one door from the sauna room, a tiny window.

I stare into the flames; I stare so hard my eyes deceive me. At one point I'm convinced I see Alice inside—in the flames I see her image, her arms spread wide and her head thrown back, her hair on fire. It seems like the flames part within and I see Jake approach and embrace her, then they both turn to look at me. Alice raises an arm, flames spread from her fingertips. Then the image fades. That's the only time I scream. My baby starts kicking inside me and the heat forces me further back. The air shimmers, the dark skeleton of the building's frame appears black through the red-orange wall of the fire, then the roof falls in.

There is no time to get help, no one to turn to. Jake is the one I always depend on. Too late for the fire department and too far away. There is nothing to do but watch. The building is small, dry as tinder, in fifteen minutes just a heap of glowing coals, red and orange.

Things change so fast. With a long stick I poke among the ashes. I can see the wreck of the stove in the corner, and I can make out where the slatted benches used to be. I don't like doing this at all. My stomach turns queasy; I try not to think of what I'm looking for. Bodies, bones. Fires should give you some warning. I don't know. Maybe they fell asleep in there from the heat; maybe they were overcome with smoke. It was an old stove. I never thought it was safe. Jake was always pouring water over the rocks on it—what if it exploded this time? But I would have heard that, wouldn't I? Suddenly warm saliva floods the back of my throat; I drop the stick and squat down, hold my belly and vomit. Then I get up and look some more. There doesn't seem to be anyone there. I step back. Six feet from the smoking ruin the ground is still soggy under my feet.

I decide to get Matt but when I reach his place I'm too tired to walk up the steep path to his house. So I pull Brittany and Christopher onto my lap, cover their ears as best I can, and lean on the horn. Matt comes running down fast, and I can tell from the way he's moving that he's mad, but when he recognizes the truck he changes a little, and closer, when he recognizes me, he starts to look worried. I tell him what I know and he jumps in. The four of us bounce back to my place, Matt driving Jake's old truck faster than it's ever gone over this road. "Slow down," I tell him. "It's too late to rush."

Even in the truck's cab his feet are running and his mouth is running, reassuring me, reassuring himself. "Everything will turn out okay," he says but I don't think he believes it. "They couldn't have been in the sauna," he says and I almost tell him the vision I saw, but I don't. He doesn't slow down one bit. And when he gets near the sugarhouse he slams to a stop, leaps out and runs. I wait for him to come back. "I need a rake," he says.

When I get to the sauna he's scraping through coals and ashes. "There's nothing here," he says finally. I nod my head. Mostly I know that. "I'm convinced," he says. "Absolutely convinced of it." He looks relieved and puzzled and maybe annoyed, too—as if somehow I could have spared him this, as if somehow this were my fault.

I hand him Christopher, and we start back along the path in slow, swelling silence. The track feels overgrown, the woods on either side heavy and dense. Matt never says a word; he doesn't even offer to carry Brittany until we're more than halfway home. When we get to the cabin I ask if he wants a beer, and he answers no in a long rush—he doesn't drink beer these days; Alice doesn't like to see him drink; mostly she doesn't want to drink herself; they don't keep beer in the house anymore. Then he hears himself and stops, and after a moment he says, "Why not? Sure."

So I get us each one and we clink bottles. "I'm glad they're all right," I say. "Wherever they are."

"Where *do* you think they are, anyway?" he asks. As if I knew. All I can do is shrug. I'm as puzzled as he is. We move the children back to the playpen under the maple, and sit on a sunny patch of lawn close to the chickenhouse. I can't look at it without seeing the black skeleton of the sauna. We sit there brooding for a long time, watching Christopher and Brittany. After a while I go in and get us each another beer. I'm finally starting to relax a little, but Matt isn't; he leans forward and asks, "So what *do* you think they're doing?"

I don't want to talk through this. I sip some beer, considering. You can coast for a long time on denial, believing what you want in spite of everything. I need to trust Jake. But it's more than that, I think. It's hard to make things work. "Probably they just went for a walk," I say at last. He shakes his head. He opens his mouth, almost speaks, then closes it again. I know I don't want to hear this. I don't want this suspicion nurtured, denial to doubt, a growing thing. I look at him resentfully. But finally I ask, "Well, what do *you* think they're doing, Matt?"

Then he doesn't answer. He just puts his arm around me. After a while I lean my head on his shoulder. "Could be anything," he says at last. "I really don't know."

We're sitting like that when Jake and Alice finally come out of the woods. They're both high as kites—smiling, singing, holding hands. Jake is celebrating the spring. He doesn't have the slightest idea that the sauna house has burned down. Alice is giggling and I notice she doesn't meet Matt's eyes. Her clothes look rumpled. I'm very glad they're all right, but I guess I knew they would be. The worry remains, though; only its focus has changed. I'm not worried about *them* anymore; now I'm worried about *us*. "Hey, why are you so gloomy?" Jake says. "It's spring, can't you dig it?"

"I thought you might be dead," I say to him. "For a while I thought you were dead." I look at Alice—she's stopped giggling but she won't meet my eyes either.

"The sauna burned down," Matt says.

"Far fucking out," says Jake. He's definitely off balance.

"Patti thought you were in it."

"Nope," says Jake. "We're fine." Then he insists on going over to look.

"Forget it," I say. "Matt's already checked. It's gone."

"But the fire," he says. "The woods."

"There isn't any fire," Matt says. "The woods are wet; the fire's out."

"Well, I have to check," Jake insists.

"We raked through the coals, Jake," I say. "Looking for you."

That sinks in—for once he seems at a loss for words. "I'm sorry," he says finally.

"Where were you, anyway?" I ask.

"It was too nice for a sauna, so we just went for a walk in the woods."

I glance at Matt, but he's looking at Alice, his face full of question and accusation and relief all smashed together. For the first time she meets his eyes directly; for a long moment they stare at each other silently, then she shakes her head no. "I'll bring you home," Matt says. Alice nods, then goes to pick up Christopher.

Jake looks around for some gesture. "I'll finish the chickenhouse," he says at last.

"Yeah," I say. "You can do that." And more besides, I'm starting to realize. We need to talk, Jake. We're outgrowing our space here.

CHAPTER 12

Killing

Matt

Winter came early their third year together, the snows steady and thick, and well before Christmas the woods were deep with it. The mountain looked brilliant in sunshine, all white and blue, deciduous trees black and finely skeletal, evergreens dark and heavy. In the deeryard soft corpses littered the snow, doe and yearling randomly scattered where they'd been dragged down and killed. Hoofprints and pawprints and great ragged trenches gouged the surface where they died, tendons ripped and throats torn. The snow was dotted with blood, sprayed with it, pink and dark red, and where the animals had bled for the longest time, almost black. Matt jammed his poles through the icy crust, stripped off his gloves and pulled them down over the grips. He squatted down on his skis and put his chin in his hands, shaking his head. The dog had gone mad with blood, just as Liza said he would.

Matt had followed Lancelot's tracks from his pen to the top of the last meadow, then into the woods on an old logging road. It had snowed a few more inches the night before, and the skiing was easy coming up the fields, just enough powder on the crust for his skis to grip. But shortly into the woods Lancelot had turned off the roadway, and Matt had to herringbone and sidestep up the steep wooded slopes. He should have come on snowshoes; several times he had to take his skis off to go through thick scrub and over rock ledges, and the snow was over his knees. Freezing rains following the November snows left a crust strong enough to hold Matt, if he kept his skis on, or Lancelot, as he ran across the surface. But not the deer—the deer punched through the crust with their small hooves. It was simple for Lancelot to chase them down, tear at their legs, tear out their throats. He'd killed as many as he could, for the pleasure in it, like a weasel in a henhouse.

Alice was the one who discovered the run open and Lancelot gone. Somehow the latch post had moved half an inch. Matt hadn't noticed it before; it must have happened gradually over the last couple of months, imperceptibly moved by the frost. Maybe there was a rock in the earth under the butt of the post or maybe the drainage right there was poor. Lancelot probably noticed it, though, tuned into the infinitesimal nuances of change, day after day in the twelve-by-eighteen run, constantly pacing the fence perimeter. Perhaps the change seemed stunning to him; his world was so small and constant now.

Pacing perimeters. Marriages come to that—dreams eroding, the world shrinking, the whole broad spectrum of life reduced to boundaries, limits, denials. Reduced to habit and drill, monotonous routine, and doglike incomprehension. Pacing perimeters, testing fences, looking for a way out.

Lancelot probably tested his fences every day, until finally the post had moved enough so that when he threw his hundred-pound body against the door the latch popped open and he was free—gone like a rifle shot, running half a mile before stopping, never looking back. His tracks led straight to the mountain.

Matt had a bad feeling about that—he guessed where Lancelot had gone, and what he'd find there. Still, he'd been relieved to see the tracks didn't lead up the town road toward Liza's place. He put on his old pair of waxless skis and followed the tracks toward the mountain.

Skiing across the meadows, following the single-minded line of the dog's tracks, straight as an arrow's flight, Matt thought about Liza, and wondered why he and Alice still kept Lancelot. He remembered Liza coming to their house a couple of months earlier, the night her border collie was killed.

That evening Matt returned from work as usual and found Alice distraught and Lancelot all bandaged up. She said he'd come home with a deep cut in his leg, unable to walk on it. The veterinarian couldn't figure out what had happened—it looked almost like a knife wound. "Who would want to stab Lancelot?" she'd asked.

And that night Liza had come rolling out of the dark in a fury. Alice answered the pounding on the door, and Liza started yelling even before she could ask her in. Matt came up, opened the door wider, and Liza turned on him. "Your damn dog attacked Sam today."

"Jesus, Liza. What happened?"

"He almost killed him, that's what happened."

"Oh, shit," Matt said, shaking his head.

"He's still at the vet's—probably won't make it through the night."

Matt said, "I'm sorry, Liza." He reached toward her shoulder. "Come on inside."

She shrugged off his hand before he could touch her. "I'm not coming in your house," she said, glaring and moving back a step. "Something's wrong with your dog, Matt." Matt took a deep breath, still shaking his head. *Alice's* dog. "He's the one who killed my sheep last summer."

"That's impossible," Alice said. "He's a *guard* dog for sheep."

"He's a killer, that's what he is," Liza said, whipping back toward her. "I've got a rifle, Alice. If I ever see that fucking dog around my place again, I'm going to shoot him. I should have shot him this afternoon."

"You're the one who stabbed Lancelot," Alice said.

Liza looked at her like she was insane. "I hit him with a hoe," she said. "Next time I'll kill him." Then she spun around and left. Matt started after her, but Alice held his arm.

Matt went up to Liza's house the next evening, to apologize and offer to pay the vet's bills. Alice didn't want to go; she thought Liza's dog was the one at fault—border collies were known for being high–strung and unpredictable. They argued while Matt changed out of his carpentry clothes, then all through his shower. Finally he drove over by himself. "Sam's dead," Liza said when he got there. "And your dog should be destroyed. I've already called the police." She stood blocking the doorway. "He's got a blood lust. It's going to be somebody's kid next. Maybe yours," she said. "Maybe Christopher."

The police took a routine report, and Alice kept Lancelot on a tie after that. "He's going to get shot," Matt told her later. "It's not just Liza. Killing sheep is a fatal disease for a dog to get around here."

"Kuvaszok never kill sheep," Alice answered. "That's absolutely foreign to their instincts. It was probably coyotes."

The deeryard had always seemed like a safe place, way up on the side of the mountain's south face in a protected cleft full of evergreen. Looking around the torn-up deer carcasses, Matt thought it would have been best if Liza *had* shot Lancelot that afternoon. Solve *that* problem anyway. A cheap fix, though—more patching up. Still, maybe with the leaks plugged they might have gotten to the heart of things. He crossed the mountain's shoulder and picked up another old logging road to follow home, not bothering with tracks anymore, and finally glad he had skis. The run home was long.

It was only that year that Lancelot began killing. It may have started with the small animals he was able to capture in his run—mice that came down after the stray bits of dry food, sometimes squirrels and chipmunks. Alice thought it was amusing—she told Matt he wouldn't need a cat anymore—but to Matt it seemed ludicrous, this huge beast of a dog chasing down chipmunks that weighed just a few ounces. Pathetic. Dragging home the carcasses the deer jackers left behind, rolling in the bones and rotting flesh, the fur stiff with old blood. Or maybe it did begin with Liza's sheep. There was Liza's collie, of course, right in front of her, too. And only a couple of weeks after that Lancelot managed to slip his tie one bright Sunday morning and kill most of Patti's chickens. Apparently he'd been able to stretch his collar half an inch and pull his head through it. Now these deer, like a new and expanded version of the carnage in the chicken run.

Matt remembered how scared Patti had sounded that morning; she had made no sense at all. "I'm not coming out of my house. I won't get near that dog. Send Alice down to get him."

"What dog?" he said. Lancelot was on a tie, had been continuously since he killed the border collie. "Never mind, I'll come myself; she's not here." Matt hung up the phone, confused and worried. He had pulled into Patti's place in time to see Lancelot inside the chicken pen, his bloody muzzle covered with dirt and feathers, bright red and white feathers all around him, too, and the corpses of chickens scattered all across their run. Lancelot was standing to the side of the coop's small door, his forepaws scratching at the top of the ramp. There were at least a couple of chickens still alive; Matt could hear them squalling about inside the coop. He watched in disbelief as one poked its head out. Lancelot struck as fast as a snake, grabbed its neck in his teeth and yanked the fat white body through the small opening.

He grinned up at Matt, his lips curled back, blood spread across his hairy muzzle and all over his teeth. It was like he had lost all sense of right and wrong, instinct and breeding. He was just killing for pleasure, going for the warm blood. Patti stood behind her storm door with a broom. "He turned on me, Matt," she shouted. "I tried to chase him off. He *bit* me." Matt went into the pen and grabbed Lancelot by the neck; his head was jammed into the narrow opening as he snarled and barked at the squawking chickens inside. Matt hauled the dog out of the chicken run and heaved him into the cab of his truck.

"Jesus, Matt," Patti said. "I don't believe it." She'd unlocked the door and held out her hand. There was a bruise on her forearm and the skin was punctured in two places.

Matt swore softly, put his arms around Patti and hugged her gently. Her breath sounded ragged in his ear. After a moment he said, "I'll drive you to the doctor's."

Patti pulled back slightly, looking up at him with wet eyes. "Just get your dog out of here." She was trembling.

It's Alice's dog, he thought, shaking his head. "He was tied. I don't know how he got off his lead."

Patti pushed him away with both hands. "Just get him out of here, all right? Get him out of here."

It's Alice's dog, he thought again, as he skied back from the deeryard to his house. Why do we still keep him? Things had escalated out of control; anyone could see that. Liza was right about blood lust. What next? Somebody's kid? Christopher?

Christopher. Sometimes Matt felt Christopher was all they had left in common. Alice would deny even that—she never spoke of *our son*, always *my son*. For Alice, Christopher cleaved them apart, not together.

How could she keep a dog like Lancelot, now that Christopher was here? Even Patti wanted the dog put down now. Once Matt had asked Alice about giving him away; some farmer could use him, give him a home. Except for the part about killing sheep. Now he wouldn't wish Lancelot on anyone.

Coming down the upper fields in broad S-shaped curves, Matt remembered the way things used to be, how he and Alice and Lancelot once skied together, the great dog bounding through the snow. Alice stopped skiing last winter, though, with her pregnancy and childbirth, and after that Lancelot wouldn't stay with him. Several times Matt had to return alone. He skied by himself for about a month after that, until the day his cat Faith appeared from nowhere, a black speck in the white distance, trotting up behind him in the narrow track. Faith wouldn't go back when he told her; she followed him miles into the woods, padding along quietly in the ski's trail. She wouldn't approach Matt when he stopped, unless he squatted down and kept his skis and poles absolutely still. Matt skied for about two hours that day, and Faith returned exhausted, riding back on Matt's right shoulder. But she showed up to join him on almost every trip after that, and she always rode back the same way—matching her balance to his rhythm and stride as they covered the long level miles. This time, though, Matt skied alone, Faith locked inside the barn.

His skis hissed through the snow as he followed the fields down to the road. He thought Liza was right; there was something fatally wrong with Lancelot. Something beyond ever fixing. He realized Alice could never put the dog down. Lancelot was her first dog; she'd owned him three times as long as she'd known Matt. He thought of their arguments after the episode at Patti's: about breeding stock, bloodlines, paying five hundred dollars for Lancelot, raising him from a puppy, Alice's love for him. He was the only dog she'd been able to bring through shows to the championship level. Above all, he was the only protection she'd had as a girl.

Recently, after Matt had warned her again about the danger to children, she'd laughed and said, "Come with me." He'd followed her into Christopher's room, where Lancelot lay dozing, curled up on a braided rug in front of the crib. Matt glanced from the sleeping dog to the sleeping child; a week before he'd found one of Christopher's bears spread across that rug, pulled down from its shelf, torn and shredded and dismembered. Lancelot opened one eye and thumped his tail on the floor a couple of times. "He's a livestock *guard* dog," Alice said. "They're bred to *protect* things. He's protected *me*."

"He's a killer, Alice."

"So he killed some chickens. Any dog might do that. Do you seriously expect me to put down a dog because he's killed a couple of chickens? Come on, Matt."

"He turned on Patti. Even Patti thinks he should be put down."

"I know; she talked to me." Alice paused for a moment, chewing on her thumbnail. "She's just temporarily overreacting. We'll keep him in the run all the time from now on. He's an investment, Matt."

Matt thought of Christopher's bear. "He's a huge liability."

They'd argued several more times after that, about responsibility, and doing what was right, but the difference between them widened each time they talked. Things shift a tiny bit, half an inch, and that's enough to change everything.

Matt crossed the road and skied to the house. He knocked the snow off his skis and stood them up against the wall by the door. "He came back," Alice said, when he got inside. "I put him in the barn behind the house."

"Jesus," Matt said, spinning around and running outside without his coat.

Lancelot had cornered Faith in the barn loft—it was incredible that he could have climbed the steep stairs, almost like a ladder. He had the cat securely in his mouth, whipping its body all around. Faith's claws were locked deep into his muzzle. When Lancelot saw Matt he stood stock still, only his masseters moving, his heavy jaws contracting, and the cat screamed, looking straight into Matt's eyes.

Matt kicked the dog hard in the side, but he only grunted and shook the cat, growling deep in his throat, turning toward Matt and turning away, his head low. Then Matt had an opening and he kicked Lancelot solidly between his back legs. The dog howled a high shriek and dropped Faith. When Matt picked her up she was already dead.

Lancelot was heading down the loft stairs. "You son of a bitch," Matt shouted, and gave him another huge kick, sending him flying down the steep stairway to crash at Alice's feet. Lancelot got up and started past her, unsteady and yelping. Matt flew down the stairs after him, still holding Faith.

"Are you crazy?" Alice yelled, grabbing his shoulder. Matt shook her off, thrust Faith into her arms, and ran out the door after Lancelot, who was heading down the hill toward the kennel and the road. "If you hurt him I'll never forgive you," she shouted.

He didn't bother to answer.

This time Lancelot's tracks did go up the town road toward Liza's place. Alice's keys were in her car, and Matt jumped in. He gunned the car forward, even as he saw Alice in the rear view mirror, running up fast behind him, shouting at him to stop.

Lancelot was just a few hundred yards down the road. He recognized Alice's car, turned and wagged his tail tentatively. For a moment he looked right into Matt's eyes, and Matt saw the eyes of the dog he once skied with, but he also saw Faith's eyes, Patti's eyes, Christopher's eyes, and he pressed down on the accelerator. At the last moment Lancelot leapt to one side, but he was too trusting, too late, and the car clipped him. Looking in the rear view mirror Matt could see him mortally wounded, struggling to rise, still staring at him, his eyes disbelieving, Alice's eyes. Matt closed his own eyes and carefully backed up, gritting his teeth, feeling the wheels bump twice. Then he put the car in first gear and slowly drove forward.

CHAPTER 13

Taking Back What's Mine

Alice

I take a breath, I close my eyes, I start my final move. Nothing can stop me now. I've made love on this spread a hundred times, and always with Matt. But this time it's Jake I slide my body toward, Jake and whatever *I* will become. My hand glides over the worn blue fabric; my fingertips touch his leg. I make the mistake of glancing down, though, and I picture Matt between us on the folded futon. That makes me pause. That makes me furious. His image woven into the threadbare cloth as if he were a part of it, fabric framing his face as if he belonged there. But he *doesn't* belong there. That's the whole point. He's *not* a part of things anymore.

I narrow my eyes; I burn right through that vision. *I* made this spread, cut and joined the sturdy cloth for our marriage bed. And I'll cut it again, tear out the seams; I'll sew a new one. Things unravel, and sometimes you have to start over.

So now it's Jake I press against, Jake, with his eyes and mouth and hands alive, his talk about loving, his smell of woodsmoke, his fingers kneading my thigh, fingers eager and hungry. His eyes are on fire, words flow like blood, his mouth is a well. I drink from his mouth, suck in his words. I want them all, and more than that. I want *him*, his body strong beside me, and I want his soul. I drink deeper and deeper. I want to swallow him with my lips and tongue, my mouth and throat. And then I *am* consuming him—suddenly, entirely— kissing him furiously now, gulping him down. I can't stop myself, and his hands are all over me. Yes. I want his body strong inside me. He unfastens the top few buttons of my shirt. I reach behind and unhook my bra. His fingers slide up my leg. Yes. With one hand I unsnap my jeans; I push down the zipper. Yes. I want this back.

There is no warning at all. The younger dogs half dozing at my feet—they don't even blink an eye until Matt unlatches the door; cold air blasts it against the wall. *Then* they bark, jumping up confused and embarrassed. Matt stamping snow off his feet, entering backward, pulling the Christmas tree in. Jake pulling his hand out. I pull my shirttails across my lap, quickly button my front, bra still loose and tangled over my breasts. Jake is already off the couch and halfway to the door, wiping his hand on the side of his leg, tripping over dogs, blocking Matt's view the whole way. Matt never turns around, though; the tree is wedged in the doorway. As Christopher wakes and starts to cry, Jake says, "Let me give you a hand with that, brother."

I zip up my pants, as quietly as I can. I call "Hi, Matt," as cheerfully as I can. I go get Christopher from his still unfinished room behind the greenhouse.

When I return, nursing Chris, Jake and Matt stand apart from each other, drinking beer in the cold light. Together they've moved the futon aside; they've put the Christmas tree in its place. The sun's attitude is low now—tonight is the solstice—and the light coming through the bank of south windows is thin and weak, illuminating the stone floor without warming it. Both men are quiet, and the music I'd put on, Vivaldi's *Winter*, sounds ominous in a way it never has before.

"Merry Christmas," Matt says. He walks over and kisses me, leaning across the top of Christopher's head. He kisses me three times before he bends down to his son. "And how is the little man?" he says, rubbing the side of his index finger against Christopher's fat cheek, cheeks like bellows, pumping in and out with that fixed intensity of nursing.

Jake leaves as soon as he finishes his beer, saying something about Patti, something about Christmas.

I look at Matt and all that I cannot understand. Touch of friends and lovers and children. All of these layers to penetrate, concentric defenses to breach. What is waiting at the center, of course, is just me. At the core of it all, just me alone.

I sit on the blue futon with Christopher dozing against my chest, full of my milk, eyes closed, spittle on his chin. I look at the Christmas tree but smell the sweet odor of him, my son, Christopher, baby and milk, flesh of my flesh. Then I smell the tree, the outside inside; I'm not sure I like it.

The scent of the fir fills the room, mingling with the humidity from the greenhouse. The air feels wet and oppressive, and Christopher feels unexpectedly sticky against me; I feel sticky and suddenly dirty. I take Christopher to his room, dust him with powder, and put him down with his pacifier stuck firmly in his mouth. I feel increasingly dirty, and in the small room adjacent to his I pump water into the tub, build a fire in the water heater. I sit in the rocker in Christopher's room, waiting for the water to warm, watching my son. He is quiet again, falling asleep again, like the dogs who have followed me in.

When Jake came bearing gifts, really I felt nothing special. I shushed the dogs and let him inside. "Sit down," he said, "I brought something for you." And from his shirt pocket he withdrew a dark maroon bag, crushed velvet, old and soft. And inside, the crystal, a large chunk of jagged quartz, a healing stone.

I hear Matt open and close the door of the gas refrigerator, hear him unsnap the top of another can of beer. I walk back into the great room. He is sitting on the futon, drinking beer and turning the great rough crystal over in his hands. "Nice," he says, "but cloudy." He holds it up to the light. "There's a fracture running right through the middle of it."

"It's a Christmas present from Jake," I say.

He looks at me, nodding his head. "From Jake," he says, then suddenly, "Let's make love."

"Don't, Matt," I say, quickly angry, and then, "We've already discussed this." A thousand times. We've been around and around and around this one, Matt, and always we come back to the same place.

"Just try..." he begins.

But I've tried my whole life. Tried to get past that endless childhood, nighttime visits from the good Uncle Louis. And I think I might have, or could have—but nine months of pregnancy, followed by childbirth. *You* try, Matthew. Try rape. Try pregnancy, childbirth. Try those on. I look at him. "You'll never understand."

Even *I* don't understand. All the confusion that followed the birth—Matt's dull insistence, Jake's relentless want, even Mona's. Mine. I think I even got past that, too. But then Lancelot, in cold blood. I'll never get over that. My only friend, my protector, ground into the dirt. That's the one I cannot get past, Matthew.

He looks at me, his eyes pleading. "Let's make love," he says again.

I say my dog's name.

Matt is silenced for a moment, then, "Are we going to spend the rest of our lives never making love?"

I don't answer. I don't know if I've ever made love. Maybe a long, long time ago.

"So you'll just never make love with me again?"

I look at him. He's getting closer.

"But you would with others."

"I don't know, Matt."

"Alice..." he starts again. Matt and his long suffering face. He doesn't know the first thing about suffering. He only cares about one thing—this thing between my legs. As if he could resurrect something there. I slowly shake my head no. I am so tired of this. Then he asks what he's really been thinking: "What were you and Jake doing when I came home?"

I turn away. "Talking," I say. I turn back. "Christ, Matt. You're so suspicious. So paranoid sometimes."

He snorts like an animal, the wuffing noise a deer will make when it senses something out of place. "You two looked like high school kids caught making out." He drains his beer. "What *were* you doing?" He puts the crystal down on the floor, the empty can next to it; he lights a cigarette. I don't answer. He inhales a deep breath, then blows it out toward me. The smoke mingles with the humid air, blocks out Christopher's scent and the smell of the tree. The stone floor is cold under my feet.

What *was* I doing? I don't know how to answer. Sometimes the ache still remains. Sometimes I get lonely, Matt. I was touched when Jake gave me the crystal. I turn and go back to my bath. Matt gets up, but doesn't follow—I hear him get another beer from the refrigerator.

I am taking off my clothes by the clawfoot bathtub when Matt comes in. His eyes are unreadable. He embraces me roughly. I twist away. He pulls me back, holds me tightly, forces his mouth over mine. His mouth tastes like beer; his tongue makes me gag. I try to push him off, but he's holding me too closely and I can't get any leverage against his chest. He slides a hand down my back, under my panties; he forces his finger inside me. And it slips in easily, my body still moist; at that moment I hate it for its betrayal. He moves his other hand toward my breast and in that instant I shove him as hard as I can; he hits the wall, my underpants rip and I push by him, free.

He follows me out into the great room, coming up fast. I see the crystal lying large and sharp on the blue vastness of the futon's cover and grab it; I turn and raise it over my head. Matt seizes my wrist, twisting flesh around bone. The crystal is heavy in my hand, my hand suddenly numb. For a moment we stare at each other in disbelief. Then he wrenches the quartz out of my grip and throws it down hard onto the stone floor; it shatters completely. Still holding my wrist, he spins around, and with his other hand rips the cover off the futon. Sun-faded and weakened, it tears too.

133

He yanks the futon off its frame, then pushes me down backward onto it. Again our eyes lock and we stare at each other with utter disbelief, absolute strangers to each other and ourselves and then he is on top of me.

And then he isn't my husband anymore. I don't have to look at his face to know that—Matt becomes Louis. And I go back to a place I haven't seen since childhood, a small cave I've always known about where there is only me, the child I never was. The opening so small only I can wiggle through it, pulling branches and leaves over the entrance to seal it off. Inside it's so tiny I have to pull my knees to my chest, wrap my arms around my legs. I curl up in darkness and wait there until it's over.

Each time he withdraws a little, I want him to keep withdrawing, all the way out. I want him to withdraw to another planet. I'm done. I've had it. When *he* is done he rolls over on his back, eyes closed, spent. He looks like he's dead. I've seen dogs do that trick better.

"Your idea of a good time," I say, standing up immediately. "Merry Christmas, Matt."

"I'm your husband," he says.

"I don't think so," I answer.

Matt's sperm inside me once more, swimming up the dark canal, cruising the salty uterine sea, looking for something to connect to. *I'm* looking for something to connect to.

So this is my Christmas present to you. Not exactly freely given. He reaches up and puts his hand on my leg, gentle now. "I'm sorry," he says. "I love you," he says.

"Jesus," I say, backing away. I can feel him start to leak down my leg. I don't know what love is, but I know it's not this.

He starts to get up. "Down," I say. "Stay down." Like commanding a dog. I've taken all his power now. It's all inside me now. Believe me, Matthew—I tell you I'm done. I stare him into place.

Believe in disaster, Matthew, and never forget: I am Alice Bourne. Remember my name. I am the reason for that poem you liked, that child of yours, those hopes you had. Alice Bourne, Matthew: body and blood. The reason dreams shrivel and die. Whisper your dreams, Matthew. I am Alice Bourne, and I will never forgive you.

"I'm sorry," Matt says again. I ignore him. I walk over to where the crystal lies shattered on the floor, pick up the two biggest pieces of quartz I can find and try to put the fragments together. But I can't get them to fit. Matt sits behind me, apologizing from the futon. "Talk to me, Alice," he says. But I am done talking. I keep my back to him. I will never say another word. I walk out of the room, a piece of broken quartz heavy in each of my hands.

CHAPTER 14

Two Wings of a Bird
Alice

Shadow darkened her son's face. Alice glanced up
from the changing table and saw the twelve-volt lights flicker
and dim. Her glance swept past the towers of black water
drums, over the raised beds of mustard greens and shungiku
and broadleaf cress. She looked beyond the vines of the tomato
plants, more than a year old now, a dozen feet long and tied to
the steep greenhouse rafters. The light continued to fade.
Through the slanted translucence of the fiberglass glazing,
Alice could just make out the low unbroken leaden-gray cloud
cover. Another cold front had stalled over them. Soon it would
begin to snow again. She closed her eyes and thought, this
doesn't work; none of this works: not the electric panels, not
the solar house, not the self-sufficient homestead, not these
long winters, not this marriage with Matt. The pall spread over
everything.

"Don't use the electric lights during the daytime," he
suggested earlier that morning. "Let the panels replenish the
battery pack."

"More than the battery pack needs to be replenished
around here," she'd answered sharply. Her anger betrayed
her—she hadn't wanted to return to Karme-Choling in the
middle of another argument. She especially didn't want to start
another argument about sex.

"Well, that's why you're going, isn't it? To replenish
yourself?"

"I don't *know* why I'm going. I need some answers."
She noticed his leg muscles flex and relax as he climbed the

137

loft stairs. They hadn't had sex for months now; they hadn't made love for over a year. Sex was such a test of things, while lovemaking had become a memory, some faded empty promise.

Coming down, Matt said, "Well, I hope you find some." He put her suitcase next to her sleeping bag by the door. "I could use some answers myself."

She watched his face settle into familiar horizontal lines—resentment flattened his eyebrows, his forehead's creases, the curve of his smile. She shook her head. It was the same tired accusation: Christopher was the reason they'd grown apart from each other.

Alice had her hands on her hips; she let out a long breath. *Christopher and everything else, Matthew. You know the litany: The trailer in Bourne Hollow. Uncle Louis.*

"Ah, Alice. It used to be fun."

Pregnancy, marriage, childbirth. Then your rape, Matthew, your rape. Not to mention Lancelot. "Used to be," she said.

Matt was still at the door, putting on his insulated carpenter's overalls and workboots. He pulled on his coat and knit hat. "I'll bring these down to the car for you," he said finally. "Then I've got to go to work." He crossed the floor and embraced her. She stiffened slightly, then hugged him back. "Don't worry so much," he said. "Don't worry about Christopher. He'll be fine." Then he was out the door and gone, walking down the path carrying her things, never looking back.

Now she picked up her son's legs with one hand and slid the diaper out with the other, wiped his bottom, saying, "pink, plump," automatically as she gave each fat cheek a final stroke and Christopher laughed, his spittle overflowing his lip.

She unfolded a new diaper and pushed it under him. *Don't worry so much.* Alice shook her head. She was convinced that before anything could be fixed you had to accept it was broken. And then find the reason why it was broken. That was the key thing—finding the reason why, the root cause.

She finished changing Christopher and picked him up. Matt was never there anymore. At night he worked late, or went to rod-and-gun club meetings, or, more recently, meditation sessions with Mona. He'd even started yoga classes now. Anything. Almost every night he had some reason not to be home. She was becoming a single parent, and discovering she liked it—simple unequivocal love. Alice wrapped her arms around Christopher and hugged him tightly to her chest. "Little Chris." Still, her eyes were moist. He looked up at her and smiled.

She carried him through the greenhouse into the main room, which Matt called the great room, although it had grown suffocatingly small that winter. She put Christopher in the canvas seat hung from the loft beam by a lengthy coiled spring. It was adjusted so his feet just touched one end of the long table top. He immediately began to jump up and down. The familiar rhythmic bouncing boinging sound filled the room as Alice pumped water into a pan to warm his bottle. She wondered if Matt was having an affair with Mona now. She'd seen the way they watched each other, out of the corners of their eyes, like cats. She put the pan on the gas stove and stoked the wood stove and turned on the two gas lamps. The room still seemed dark and small so she took five candles down from the shelf over the sink and placed them on the opposite end of the heavy table that Matt built out of soft dark five-quarter pine (for his first wife, it turned out). She gave Christopher his bottle and made a cup of tea for herself, comfrey that she'd grown herself in the large garden they had instead of some suburban lawn.

Alice sat down in front of the candles, looked at her watch and drummed her fingers on the table. She still couldn't understand why her marriage was failing. At first she thought it was destiny—Louis, abuse as a child. Although whenever she'd discussed that with Matt he couldn't confront it. He'd say, "But that's all over. That's all over now." And early that winter she'd realized he was right, in a way—that it *had* been over, but only for a little while.

Early that winter Alice had gone to Karme-Choling for
the first time. They had all gone up together—Matt and Alice,
Christopher, Mona—three hours up the Connecticut River
valley to a nineteenth-century village on the Vermont side with
a wooden church and general store, some white houses around
a green—so traditionally Protestant it ached. The retreat was
situated outside of the village on an abandoned hill farm. They
arrived in moonlight, and Alice's first impression was of
incongruity, an imperfect fusion of New England and Tibet.

They stood for a moment in the snow outside, Matt
holding Christopher, Mona with one arm around Alice, her
other around Matt. The original farmhouse was still covered
with white clapboards, but the trim had been painted bright red,
and yellow banners with red symbols hung from a rank of poles
in the dooryard. Wood-framed additions for kitchens and
dining rooms extended behind the farmhouse, turned and
continued as dormitories, libraries, meeting rooms, small shrine
rooms, then turned again to end at the meditation hall, a single
room bigger than the entire original house. A meditation
garden, covered with snow, separated these wooden arms. The
gable of the meditation hall was fitted with a massive red and
gilt symbol, the Buddhist knot of compassion.

Inside, instead of gongs and incense or monks with
shaved heads and saffron robes, Alice found a credit card
machine on the front desk, and steel file cabinets all along one
wall. The people there were all Westerners, as ordinary as she
was, except that the men all wore business suits, even at ten at
night, in the winter, in Vermont. Mona was hugging people.
Matt showed off their son. Alice filled out some forms.

When she went deeper into the building, the rugs, wall
hangings, symbols and ornaments all became more esoteric,
and at first she'd nudge Mona, point and smile, but as she
passed portrait after portrait of famous teachers and
Bodhisattvas, all men, all framed in gilt, she said to Mona,
"Where are the women?" more loudly than she intended. Matt
looked at her. She felt embarrassed. Then she became embarrassed by her own embarrassment.

Mona said, "You don't have to love the messenger."

There was a pervasive sense of compassion, awareness, presence. She felt it in the quiet way people listened to
her, in their gently deliberate answers. It was all comfortable
and uncomfortable; the pieces didn't perfectly fit. She glanced
at Mona, who looked as if she had come home.

Alice spent those days in sequestered lectures and long
meditation sessions. She finished the first evening meditation
feeling very tired and profoundly alone. She missed Christopher, and that night she dreamed about him, and all the next
day as she dozed on her cushion she dreamed about him, too.
The second night Alice was so determined not to fall asleep
during the talk that she sat directly before the speaker, thinking
that embarrassment would keep her awake, but it didn't.

A singular thing happened to Alice at the very end of
the third day. During that final meditation she sensed, for the
first time, the space that Mona had so often described. Her ego
disappeared—for a moment she was free of her name. She
didn't know how long it was gone. She didn't even notice it
was gone until it had already returned, suddenly reclaiming her
consciousness and demanding explanation.

She tried to understand what had happened. In
retrospect it felt like melting, a steady diminishing of self.
She'd become increasingly removed as the layers of ego lost
substance and dissolved. She'd become a watcher. Awareness
grew and shrinking continued, until her ego became infinitely
small, the merest point in space and time—then it disappeared
altogether. What remained, or was revealed, was awareness
without name. And for a moment Alice *was* that awareness,
except the *Alice* was gone.

A moment later she decided that was all backward.
Her ego's disappearance was really the result of an immense
expansion. The growing awareness had inexorably filled her
shell of ego, smoothly burst it, and expanded so far beyond the
broken fragments of self that her shattered ego—that artful
deception—wasn't even remembered.

It was hard to pin down exactly. Already her ego was solidifying with a stunning, desperate speed, instantly refilling her mind with more than she could manage. The same old thoughts distended her consciousness, clotting everything and leaching out like thickening waste. But it was too late. For a brief, shining moment the artifice had been revealed, and once was forever.

More important than that, she realized Louis was inextricably bound to her ego. And she also understood that, not only *could* she escape Louis, once she already *had*. In the beginning with Matt she'd been free of all that—their first night with each other, those first months they shared, their wedding, building the house together. *We had it all, Matthew. For a moment we were there.*

Alice became aware of Christopher bouncing and boinging. She leaned over and kissed him, then got up from the table, crossed the room, and pulled down a carton from on top of the propane refrigerator. Thinking again that only a man could design a house without closets, she emptied its contents onto the table—the house plans and her pictures and the bits of journal writing she kept.

She looked for the pictures of the two of them starting the house the summer before last, building the very space where she now sat. It seemed so magical then, all the bright white pine and the fresh clean smells of cut wood. There were pictures from last summer, building the room behind the greenhouse for Christopher. For months last fall it remained almost finished, but not quite ready, so it couldn't be used at all, which was typical.

There were pictures of Matt building the floor now under her feet, with fieldstone they'd picked themselves. For a year Matt had noted stones and rocks on the property. He named them, saying, "This one would be perfect in front of the threshold. A doorstone. Remember this one—it will be good in front of the stove. A hearthstone. The quartz streaks in this one are beautiful—we can use it as a centerpiece. Have others radiate out from it."

They spent two days driving around the property in Matt's pickup collecting them all. He drove to a place on the brook and washed each stone with a wire brush before he brought them to the house. They made a small hill next to the door, but Matt said they needed more, and they spent a whole week picking through the old fieldstone walls on their place, selecting the flattest rocks and loading them into the back of the truck.

They were part of the thermal mass. Twelve tons of it: eight tons of dirt and four tons of rock. Matt had calculated it all out the previous winter.

Matt laid down an unbroken sheet of plastic on the raked subsoil, then two layers of foam insulation board, brilliant white, two foot by eight foot sheets, the joints carefully staggered, then another unbroken sheet of polyethylene, then eighteen inches of dirt. He worked for three days bringing in the dirt, cutting away a high spot of the brook's bank, trundling the wheelbarrow along a track of two-by-twelves, lumbering down the gentle slope to the house, up over the planks crossing the threshold. Alice raked each load of the dark clay smooth over the clear plastic and stark white foam. She danced around on top of it with close hopping steps, tamping it down while Matt returned for more. The fat pneumatic tire bounced across the boards on the empty trip back; it was squashed almost flat and seemed to roll sideways when he returned with the wheelbarrow fully loaded.

Matt spent two days laying the rocks out in careful patterns on the floor. "We're way behind schedule on this," he'd say. He worked long into the night with strings and levels, a shovel and crowbar, arranging rocks in the light of a Coleman gas lantern. When he finally crawled into bed late on the second night, Alice hugged him. "I'm done," he said. "They're all laid out. God. It took forever." He stretched his back. "Everything takes five times longer than it should." Alice took him in her arms, but he fell asleep before they could make love.

The next morning he went to work and Alice returned
to the house site. The stones all rocked where Matt had laid
them, and she decided not to stain the trim boards as he had
suggested. Instead, she took the wheelbarrow out of the shed.
One of the handles was repaired with a length of two-by-four,
rough and too large to be comfortable in her hand. It took her
almost fifteen minutes to load the heavy clay, and she was tired
and sweating despite the early morning chill when she discovered she couldn't lift the full wheelbarrow. She had to shovel
half of the dirt out again before she could raise the handles and
start toward the house. On the first trip the thick tire ran off the
narrow track and sank in the soft ground, spilling the load.
Alice dragged additional planks to the track and doubled its
width. On the second trip she lost control of the wheelbarrow
on the gentle slope. It outran her, smashed into the wall of the
house, broke one of the new siding boards, and spilled. She
learned to push down on the handles and use the legs as brakes,
and she brought the third load to the door, but as she tried to
push it up the planks over the threshold, the weight shifted, the
wheel pushed the planks apart sideways, the wheelbarrow
dropped to its axle, and the load tipped over.

Alice shoveled the dirt over the threshold and with a
stiff broom swept the dirt into the spaces between the stones.
She used a piece of one-by-three firring strip to tamp it down
hard between the rocks. She'd tried the iron crowbar—as the
solar house books recommended—but it was too heavy to
wield with accuracy. The floor was eighteen by twenty feet and
she worked without stopping for lunch. By dinnertime she was
finished. She was sweeping the floor clean when Matt drove
up. Still covered with dirt and sweat, she walked down to
where he parked. The truck bed was full of bags of cement.

"Hey. I stopped at the apartment for dinner but the
troops had abandoned the fort."

"Sorry. I didn't realize how late it was. I needed to
finish this job I was doing."

"Overworked and underfed," he said. He hugged her. "You sure are dirty. Did you stain the trim?" He hoisted an eighty pound bag of cement to his shoulder with a grunt.

"No. I was working on a surprise for you." Taking his free hand she led him up to the house without further explanation. She opened the door smiling. Matt set the mortar down by the broken siding board, looked at it but didn't say anything.

He was silent, too, as he looked through the doorway. Her floor stretched in front of them, the dirt and stone uniformly level. She watched him step out onto it. The stone under his foot was solid and didn't rock. He took another step.

Alice's smile felt like it might split her face. "See what I did? I spent all day finishing this. I brought in seventeen loads. All by myself."

Matt looked all around, his expression truly dumbfounded. "Why did you *do* this?" he said finally.

Suddenly her smile hurt. "Well, so *you* wouldn't have to. Every stone rocked, Matt. I brought in *seventeen* loads of dirt. I had to pack it in between every single stone. Now it's solid. What's the problem?" She walked past him, tired and slow.

"I can't believe it. This will all have to be dug out."

"What are you talking about? I did a good job. This is every bit as good as that greenhouse floor we saw—the bricks packed in sand. It's better than that."

"God, Alice. I'm so tired. I've been working all day long. I rushed to the yard so I could get cement before they closed." He walked over to the far wall. "I wanted to get a quick dinner and use the daylight to finish the floor." Matt slid his back down the wall and sat on the floor. "I'm so tired."

"But that's why I did it. So you wouldn't have to."

"Alice. Why do you think I washed all the stones so carefully?" She didn't say anything. She closed her eyes. "It was so cement would stick. Why do you think I was so careful to set them on *top* of the dirt? Every stone two inches apart?" Alice kept her mouth closed. She shook her head. "It was so

there'd be *room* for the mortar, so all the joints would be the
right size." Matt drew his legs up, folded his arms across his
knees and rested his head on his arms. He sighed. "I can't
believe it." He raised his head and rested it against the wall
behind him, looking at the high pitched ceiling. "Alice. All
that dirt will have to be dug up and taken out. Every damn
stone will have to be picked up, brought to the brook and
rewashed, brought back to the house and relaid." Alice looked
at him silently, clenching her teeth. "Why didn't you just stain
the trim like I asked you to?"

"Why didn't you just tell me you'd decided to cement
the floor?" She felt tears in her eyes and they made her more
angry; she shook and they began to streak down her cheeks,
feeling sticky in the grime there.

"Now you're crying. God, I'm the one who should be
crying. I can't believe I have to do this all over again. Why
don't you just do what I tell you to do?"

"Because I'm not some...*dog* that you can just order
around."

Matt looked levelly at her. "I'll be here all night,
Alice. Four tons of stone." She walked by him and out the
door. "Where are you going?"

"Home."

She waited up for him until almost midnight. Before
she fell asleep she taped a note to the bathroom mirror: "Your
dinner's in the oven."

The next picture was a little older, a delayed exposure
Alice took two summers ago, the day they'd finished closing
the main house to the weather. The photograph showed them
holding hands by the open front door, looking at the camera,
raising glasses of champagne. They wore leather nail aprons,
with twenty ounce framing hammers slung low on their hips
like gunfighters' pistols. It was shortly after she'd become
pregnant.

It had started to rain soon after that picture was taken,
and they'd gone inside, bringing the champagne with them. In

146

the loft Matt unrolled the sleeping bag they kept there for lovemaking. "This is the first time we'll make love *inside* our house," he said. "Closed in."

She smiled and hugged him. She used to tell him it felt like they were perched within the skeleton of some dinosaur, among bare posts and beams, timbers in space. The rain beat on the roof and walls, windows and doors. She kissed him. "I liked it before—with the deck down but no walls up—it was like floating in air. But this is *really* nice, Matt," she said, and snuggled her head into his chest.

Matt lay on his back, naked after lovemaking, and Alice poured out the last of the champagne. He said, "If we can do this, we can do anything."

"Build a house?"

He took the glass she offered. "The magazines are full of stories of couples who split up halfway through. It's just too hard." He raised the glass in another toast. "To you. To us. We're special."

"Jesus, Matt, if you knew that, why did you want us to build a house together?"

He took her hand. "Because we really *are* special. *We* can do it."

After a minute Alice said, "What if we're not special? What if we're just regular people?"

He kissed her eyes. "You think too much, Alice." He kissed the answer forming on her lips.

Alice wiped her eyes and put the photograph down. *But we weren't special, Matthew. We were the same as everybody else.*

There was the master copy of the plans Matt gave her when they finally finished the main house. He drew those himself. Then there was the picture Alice took of Matt and Mona last summer. They had their backs to the camera. Mona was holding Matt's hand and pointing at something in the distance, beyond the frame of the photograph.

Christopher finished his bottle, let it drop on the table and began reaching for the bright pictures. Alice gave them to him one by one. He put some into his mouth and chewed them, and crumpled the others.

Alice began to read her journal entries from the time Matt had persuaded her to join Mona's Buddhist study group. She had sat cross-legged in Mona's living room and learned the most basic things about meditation—posture, breath, dismissal of thought. They sat for fifteen minutes at a time. Alice would examine the pattern of the carpet at her feet, the precision of the woodworking in the cabinetry on the walls—pieces more perfectly cut and fitted than Matt's work. She would become aware of the storms without, the peace within, the warmth of the fire and the ticking of Mona's clocks.

At first, Alice thought meditation was an impossible waste of time. It was an old person's enterprise, contemplating life from its conclusion. There was no time for it now, not with a child to raise. But she kept going back; the peacefulness attracted her, and the possibility of understanding. Ultimately she accepted it, the Hinayana Path, the narrow way: mindfulness, awareness—two wings of a bird. Freedom of flight and vision that saw everything. But even with meditation, she still could not understand *why* her marriage was failing. The root cause.

Over the winter she'd talked to her friends, Matt's friends; she'd talked to Matt's mother and to the minister who married them and whose church she once attended. She even tracked down Matt's ex-wife and talked to her.

She became convinced that the failure didn't stem from Christopher. Pregnancy and childbirth—everyone went through that. It wasn't even Matt's rape, not even the killing of her dog—as major as those things were, they were still symptoms. What she couldn't comprehend was why, and how, Matt became Louis. When she distilled out all that winter's talk what she was left with was her original question—why—maybe more polished somehow, as if from use, but still unanswered.

Alice closed her journal, Matt's voice in her head. *Don't worry so much. You think too much, Alice, that's what the problem is.* There was a knock from outside announcing Mona's arrival. Alice dried her eyes and opened the door. It had started to snow. "I'm sorry I'm late," Mona said. "The roads are already bad. It's going to be a long trip to Karme-Choling this time." She looked at Christopher spitting up a bit of photograph. "Solid food already?"

Alice wiped his mouth and gathered the remains of the pictures together and put them back in the box. She nuzzled him and kissed him good-bye.

"Mona, I appreciate your help."

"It's okay. I'm glad for a chance to look after the little guy." Mona took off her coat. Snow began to melt on the shoulders and sleeves. "So, are you ready to go? A week of meditation. Pretty good. I wish I could do it." She looked at Alice's face. "Well, it should help you get things sorted out, anyhow."

"I'll call each night."

"Don't worry. Chris and Matt will be okay." Alice walked to the window and stood looking out. Mona said, "Be careful of the driving. It looks like we're in for a real storm."

"Look, Mona, don't sleep with Matt when I'm gone," Alice said without turning around.

The hiss of Mona's long indrawn breath was loud in the silence. "Alice, come on."

Alice turned to face her. "I mean it. You're my friend. Give us a chance to resolve this."

Mona looked at her face and then at the floor. Alice kissed Christopher for the last time. She paused by Mona, gave her a quick hug, and said, "Mona. You're *my friend*," repeating the words like a prayer chant.

It took Alice almost six hours to drive through the storm, and most of the way she worried about leaving Christopher with Mona and Matt. And maybe Matt with Mona. She was returning to an intensive practice session with a visiting

teacher, Rinpoche, to meditate for seven days in the red and
gold hall, sixteen hours at a time.

Her meals were brought to her and ritually served in
small bowls of black polished wood, eaten in silence, sitting
cross-legged on meditation cushions. Once an hour her sitting
practice was interrupted with ten minutes of walking meditation. Except for the deep hollow gong marking the change, the
silence remained unbroken.

She missed Christopher constantly, and at first that was
her only understanding. She sat with hundreds of people, a
tranquil red and yellow sea, centered in the shallow breathing
and silence. She tried to find that meditative space again, tried
to dismiss her ego, let go of herself, banish her thoughts. But
they kept creeping back. They would unreel like a film; she sat
like a moviegoer, watching the story of her life unfold.

Everything had happened so fast: meeting Matt,
becoming lovers, living together, buying land. Getting pregnant, marrying, building a home. Christopher's birth.

Alice rearranged herself on her cushion, straightening
her posture. Her thoughts drifted to last winter, the winter of
Christopher's birth. That was hard. That was where their
friendship foundered, on her insistence that Christopher come
first. That was when Matt really started to look like Louis.

No rebirth came for them *that* spring. Christopher
thrived. Hundreds of tulips Matt planted the previous fall
emerged in spectacular color. The orchard flowered, a forest of
bloom. Great clouds of white flowers hung low in the air and
showered down with the occasional wind. They had been
married in that orchard only a year earlier. It seemed like
another life.

Sometimes still she'd focus on the missing kiss, the
empty embrace, the distance between them. But after
Christopher's birth she'd never felt like making love again, and
those times Matt insisted she'd felt raped. Those mornings
she'd woken to him behind her, lain still in bed, listened to the

birds call, tried not to breathe. Finally withdrawing into the cave she'd created in childhood, that place she'd crawled into when Louis entered her bedroom at night.

Alice became aware of the woman sitting to her right. The woman was rigid. Her hair was the length and color of Mona's, but her face was hard and unfriendly. Several times during the morning's practice their eyes had met when Alice had allowed hers to roam. When Alice's eyes lit on the face of that hard woman, she flicked her own eyes sideways at Alice and frowned. Alice would quickly look straight ahead.

And think about Mona. She wondered about her as a lover, about women as lovers, loving men. Loving Matt. She made herself see Mona's body the way he did last winter, after Christopher was born, when they all started taking saunas together again. Her small breasts and flat belly.

Alice's eyes wandered over the main meditation hall. She thought of her first expectations, months ago: something Congregational, all varnished wood and white paint, or perhaps something like a vast monastic cell. Instead, everything was bright red and gilt. Gilded leaves encircled the columns, masses of gilt filled in all the corners and joints of the room, gilt symbols covered the walls. The room was unfurnished except for two shrines. The main one was an elaborate version of the shrine at Mona's: great bouquets of flowers, water, candles and incense, a large Buddha. At the side of the hall was a small raised platform with an empty chair, the teacher's chair, Rinpoche's chair, the only chair in the room. The floor was covered with hundreds of red and yellow meditation cushions. A large gong stood in one corner. The hall seemed spacious and open, and ostentatious. Her knees ached.

Letting go. Occasionally Alice would begin to feel a space being created, a mystical clear space, a letting go of her ego, some kind of freedom with its nucleus in the center of the room and expanding beyond the walls, beyond the hayfields and old pastures and the valleys and the mountains—for Alice it stopped expanding when it met the wall of her marriage.

Thinking about Matt. One evening, a month ago, Alice was meditating at home, cross-legged and erect on her red and yellow cushion, trying to empty her mind of thought. Matt came down from the loft, put his hand on her shoulder without a word, kissed the top of her head, once, slowly, with great kindness. *We almost had it, Matthew. We touched it with our hands.*

Thinking about Matt with Mona. One night, when he was late arriving home, Alice was sure she could smell Mona's scent on him. When she asked him for an explanation he said Mona had given him a back rub.

Alice shut her eyes tight, banishing ghosts, *thinking, thinking, thinking*, and she had almost dismissed Matt and Mona when the hard woman sitting next to her suddenly crumpled. Her presence just disintegrated into sobbing. A monk looked up and shouted just once, "Let it go!" His voice banged out sharp, incredibly hard and unwelcome. It seemed to Alice wholly without sympathy. She wanted to put her arms around the woman, but she didn't dare. After a long while the woman's sobs became infrequent and she straightened up on her cushion.

Alice wanted to talk to someone to understand that. But all the time was spent in silence, and that night, when she tried to talk to the woman sleeping next to her in the dormitory, the woman said, "There's no talking now. It'll make more sense later. Ask me again when we're done." And although she smiled, she wouldn't say anything more.

Three days passed before Alice began to understand the monk's response. That woman's tragedy wasn't real anymore; it was just a thought, a thought to let go of, a thought to join the others, wherever thoughts go when they leave. Like the love she had with Matt. It was her past, not her present. Letting go. It wasn't real anymore.

Still, Alice felt things were getting out of control, things had gotten out of control, everyone had let things get out of control and everyone had brought that to the hall. A sum of small parts, a collection of tragedies, a room full of disaster. The hall seemed a universe out of control. But it could be tamed. It was being tamed.

She understood that was her enlightenment.

Rinpoche held private audiences. At first Alice thought she would never meet with him. She would never perform the ritual greeting, the bows and prostrations. But after sitting for days her sense of herself eroded, and she was left with just her question—why—why marriages fail, why love is lost. Mostly she managed to sit without thinking much at all.

Time would pass and she'd be aware of nothing; she'd notice its passage only after it was gone. Occasionally she'd become aware of an amorphous sadness, as if awakening from an unhappy dream; she'd come to awareness saturated with diffuse unhappiness. Sitting, banishing thought, concentrating on her breathing, she'd try again to disappear into the space, the hollow space of her own breath, the hollow space where her thoughts used to be, where her ego, her self had been.

On the last day Alice requested her first audience. It was in a minor meditation room she had never been in before. The room was small and nondescript, with white walls and ceiling and a polished wooden floor. A small altar stood against one wall, adjacent to the door she entered through. Rinpoche sat facing the altar, utterly still, and Alice bowed slightly. He hadn't moved when she opened the door. He was an old man, and small, his hair short and wispy. She thought of a gray mouse. His face was lined but not happy or unhappy. It didn't seem particularly full of love or even warmth—it just seemed at peace. Rinpoche wore white clothes, and an orange robe of some silky fabric. At first Alice thought he was asleep, with his half hooded eyes and imperceptible breathing.

"Come in," he said. He smiled and unclasped his hands. He motioned to the empty cushion in front of him, an enveloping gesture, inviting. "Sit." Alice understood that she didn't have to bow or prostrate herself, but she did anyhow; she bent low at the waist, then knelt and touched her forehead to the floor. Rinpoche's posture and smile remained unchanged. Alice came and sat in front of him. They sat without talking for a few minutes, facing each other, breathing.

Finally he asked her name. She said, "Alice," then was silent again.

Sitting in front of him, she realized her question didn't make any sense anymore. Three times she started to ask it. The first time she suspected this man had no answer for her— he was a complete stranger; the second time she understood that any answers there were she already had; the third time she knew that, really, there was no answer. It just was.

Rinpoche smiled. "So? You have questions about your practice?"

Close up, his face looked so wise, so full of insight and understanding, that he seemed supernatural. So she blurted it out, the only thing she thought about, this thing that was happening to her without understood reason, her obsession— but her question came out as a statement: "My marriage has failed."

Rinpoche sat without moving. He nodded once more. Alice was quiet for another moment. She listened to their breathing, smelled the incense, and realized this was to be the depth of her understanding; this was her revelation: "It can't be fixed."

Rinpoche nodded once more. He smiled sympathetically. "How old are you?"

"Twenty-four."

"Um-hmm." He looked at Alice and his eyes were full of compassion. "How long have you been married?"

"Three years."

"Do you have any children?"

"We have a son. Christopher." Alice smiled at the sound of his name, then tears filled her eyes.

Rinpoche frowned slightly and shook his head. A tear spilled down Alice's cheek. "I am sorry for your suffering," he said. "Sit with me."

154

They sat in silence for several more minutes. Alice became aware again of the smell of incense, of the quiet, the peace. Rinpoche looked up once at her, studied her face, and said, "It is hard." Alice nodded and didn't say anything.

That evening Alice sought a second audience, and this time the teacher spoke first, after studying her for a long moment. He said, "I can only teach you to sit." Again they sat in silence, this time for almost an hour. Finally Alice stood, bowed, and returned to the meditation hall.

In the hall she sat peacefully, no longer trying to understand. She concentrated on her posture and her practice, and gradually the room full of meditators slipped away. She labeled her thoughts and dismissed them with her breath. Christopher. Matt. Mona. Louis. Rinpoche. Breathing out. Alice. Breathing out.

She felt larger and smaller than she ever had before, expanding and contracting like the air that filled and left her. Breathing out, she lost track of her thoughts, of her worry, and then, finally, of herself.

The meal at the end of the last night was bread and egg drop soup. Sitting in silence on her cushion, Alice thought it was the most delicious thing she had ever tasted. Looking at the strands of egg in the amber broth she felt that the answer might as well be in the soup itself, or in the eating of it, or in the appreciation of it; that there was no answer, there was no question, there was just the meal.

CHAPTER 15

The Ocean at Night

Matt

She'd left a hole in the dark, tinged with her scent, but it didn't last. Already the night was filling in behind her: sea salted breezes and the sweet smell of jasmine, and always the odor of damp, moldering earth. He followed her like a memory, down the splintered boardwalk to the beach. Her white T-shirt was all he could see ahead, pale in the starlight. At the edge of the jungle she stopped, turned, waited. Tapping her tightly rolled towel against the boardwalk railing, she said, "I've enjoyed this vacation, you know." When he got close enough she poked her towel into his bare chest. "Lots more than I thought I would."

"I'm glad." He held her shoulders lightly and kissed her, a kiss like a question. She was twenty-four; he was twenty-six; together they felt like fifty. A week earlier she'd told him she wanted to separate. Out of the overstuffed security of their counselor's plush armchair—she never chose the couch—she'd suddenly announced she wanted to leave. *Had* to leave, she added, when he looked at her. "Just some distance for awhile," she'd insisted, crossing her arms. They were silent for a moment, then she said, "I need some space," her teeth clenching down hard on the last word.

For awhile. What is separation if not a prologue, a prelude, a dress rehearsal for divorce? Space and distance forever and ever. World without end. Amen.

Hermit crabs scuttled across the rough boards behind them, the dry rasping sound of dragging claws like old bones. He tentatively touched her face, fingertips light on her temples. She broke off their kiss. "I love you," he said.

157

"I know you do."

They'd swum together that afternoon, holding hands, exploring the reefs of Francis Bay with snorkels, moving slowly among fantastic gardens in the shallows—finger coral, star and brain coral, sea whips and fans. Languid butterfly fish swam among the reefs, feeding in small groups of silver and black. Green and blue parrot fish delicately grazed. All afternoon they dove together, cruised the surface, hands touching or clasped. Staghorn coral and elkhorn coral formed stunted submarine forests in the deeper water. Thousands of minnows darted there in synchrony, glinting silver, seeming to change the available light. Schools of snapper flashed swirling yellow in the shoals. He wanted to go through life like that: with her, holding hands, skimming the surface, diving down deep, coming back up for air.

He dropped his hands. A marriage needs air. She turned and stepped out of the jungle onto the beach; she kicked off her sneakers in the sand. A huge iguana slowly lumbered off into the verge on their right, ponderous and indifferent. The long narrow crescent of beach stretched away empty in both directions, embraced at its ends by rocky outcroppings that thrust far out into the sea like arms. The air on the strand smelled like a world newborn to him, sand and ocean and rock, tinged with jasmine and frangipani. He filled his lungs with it.

She led him to the edge of the water. They walked quietly along the hard sand where the gentle waves met the beach. Their feet caused luminous splashes as they disturbed the phosphorescent algae, and the water slid down their skin with a surreal sheen. He took her hand and asked, "Do you really want to separate?"

"I think so," she said. "What choice is there?" They walked slowly; he held her hand all the way down to the southern end of the strand, to the rocks entering the sea, stony arms embracing the ocean. Where the sand met the rock she turned to him. Her hands traced down his chest to the strings of his bathing suit; her fingers untied the knot at his waist and slid the suit down his legs.

"Make love to me," she said.

"Here? In the open?"

She covered his mouth with her hand. "Here. Now. I've always wanted to make love on a beach."

You've always wanted to make love a public display, he thought. Jake and Patti and Mona—all our friends knew about our problems before I did. The committee of three. Sanctimonious judges.

She pressed her body against his, running her hands up and down his back. Then she stepped back, unknotted her shirt and tugged it over her head. Her long blond hair fell over her shoulders and chest. He kissed her. She guided his head to her breast. He thought he heard voices on the beach. She drew him down onto the sand.

The beaches of St. John were all infested with tiny fleas, stinging burns in the perfect sand. He started to scratch his legs. "Here, spread out the towel," she said. He scratched his arms. Once more he thought he heard voices. She touched him between his legs. "What's the matter?" she asked.

"There are other people on the beach."

"You're just imagining things."

"No, listen." They both heard voices approach.

"Pay attention to *me*," she said. She started to fondle him.

"They're coming this way."

"So what? It's a big beach. Stop worrying about what some strangers might think." But he stood up and pulled on his bathing suit. "You're always so concerned about everybody else," she said. When he didn't answer she pulled her T-shirt back over her head, drew her legs up to her chest and clasped her knees. For a long moment she looked out over the ocean in silence. The beach was quiet. Finally she said, "We never know, when we do things, when we're doing them for the last time."

He looked at her. "You think this is the last time we'll make love?"

"We're not making love." She drew away when he touched her. "You almost never know last things when they happen."

He knelt beside her on the towel, stroked her and smoothed her body flat. She lay tensed and didn't respond. Stretching out next to her, he placed his hand between her legs, the slight mound of flesh soft again under his fingertips. Once their counselor suggested they hold hands whenever they talked—touch would dampen anger.

His fingers settled into intimacy he used to take for granted—before pregnancy and childbirth, before exclusion and rejection. Before last Christmas, when she'd given herself to Jake. Before he'd taken her back.

Now he pushed her shirt up gently. The bottom half of her bikini was dark navy blue with beige stripes, indistinct in the night. A wide band of elastic crossed each hip, high. He slipped her bathing suit over her hips and down her legs. Her smooth buttocks were globes, the hair between her legs blond and always surprisingly hard. He bent over her and covered her back with light kisses, her hips, her thighs.

She didn't move at all. He thought of the person arrested in Albany a few months ago for fornicating with a corpse he found in an alley. He wondered if they had already made love for the last time.

The other voices came closer; he heard them distinctly. "Don't stop," she said. He kissed her mouth, her breasts, her belly, the soft cleft between her legs. She moved almost imperceptibly under his lips. The want to be wanted. He placed her hand on the back of his head. She rested it there for a moment, then let it drop. To be held. She moved slightly under his lips, otherwise she was still. Loved. Suddenly her whole body stiffened; a long drawn moan escaped. He rested his head on her belly, tasting salt and sex. She lay without moving.

They both heard the voices drift away. "See?" she asked finally. "They knew we were here, but they didn't bother us."

"I feel like I'm on trial." He lay next to her with his hand resting on the damp swelling between her legs.

She turned toward him. "Do you want to make love?"

"No. Not now."

"Is there anything you need?"

"No," he said, after a moment. There was no limit to that one. "It's all right." She closed her eyes and didn't say anything more. He watched her in the darkness as she drifted off to sleep. After a few minutes he stood up and walked slowly to the edge of the sea. The lights glowed on the mastheads far out in the bay. He strode into the water deliberately, and when it was chest high he began to swim. The sea was luminous around him; as he swam he left trails of bubbling light, foaming water, and water dripped from his arms like a lighted curtain. The ocean was dark, warm and thick with salt, molten. He put his head down into the water and lifted one arm, then another, in a strong crawl.

After a long time he stopped swimming and rolled over onto his back to rest. He drifted on the surface, watching the stars. Floating in the dark night he wondered what would become of them, all this accumulated insult and injury, this weight of weariness.

He swam slowly on his back, thinking the ocean wasn't really beautiful at night—it was deep and dark, thick and phosphorescent. Anything could live in that water. Anything could be under him right now in fact, mindlessly cruising, spinning slow circles in the black depths, sensing him up on the surface.

He rolled over and began to tread water, trying to get his bearings. The masthead lights seemed further out than before, but that was impossible; he must have drifted a considerable distance parallel to the shore. He looked all around him. There were no lights visible on the island, and he couldn't decide if he had moved north or south along the shoreline—if he should now swim left or right. Floating quietly, he listened for the sound of breaking waves, but he heard nothing. He knew if he made the wrong choice he'd swim toward the open sea. For no good reason he decided the island lay to his left, so he swam in that direction, hoping that he was indeed swimming toward shore, and his wife on the beach.

But it almost didn't matter. The ocean was dark and warm, and by now he felt comfortable in it. He could swim forever like this, on the surface of that deep water, even with all that life under him, everything at once predator and prey.

CHAPTER 16

Maybe there Never Was

Matt

At the beginning of their final summer together Matt spread out rolled roofing for the last time. The day was so hot the tar ran like water, and sweat trickled down the inside of his glasses, streaking the yellow dust there obscuring his vision. He polished the lenses again on the bottom of his T-shirt. The frames were tacky with tar now, and tar was beginning to stick in his hair. He hated this work. It was hard, mindless work—it made his back ache and his brain numb. Only his fear of falling made him pay any attention at all.

Matt cut each piece of the heavy asphalted felt on the ground, three feet wide and eighteen feet long. He rolled up the sections as tightly as he could and carried them up the ladder on his shoulder, six courses of roofing, one piece at a time. Small bits of white gravel worked loose, slipped under his shirt and stuck to his wet back. The black bundles against the side of his face smelled of hot roads and burning dumps. He thought of his promise to Alice yesterday. If you could call it that. Body language. He lit a cigarette. What had they come to? Trading carpentry for sex—that's how they'd end their marriage; that's what they'd get to remember. All the bad deals, the shabby bargains, the corruption of love. The match stuck to his finger when he shook it out.

He was already feeling displaced. Alice's kennel was the first building to go up that he hadn't actually built with his own hands. And at the last minute she had modified his design—she had Jake include a small apartment in the kennel's second story. Matt understood she would move into it soon, as

soon as she could, perhaps this fall. And perhaps by winter
she'd be sleeping there with others, maybe even Jake, who was
doing most of the building now.

Yesterday Matt had been talking to Alice by the little
springhead brook behind the house. He lay shirtless on young
grass, watching the stream spill gently over the top of the
wooden crib dam he'd recently built. Christopher slept on a
plaid blanket behind them, away from the water pooling back
from the notched logs. Matt had settled him there with his
bears, soothed him to sleep with a story. After a silence Alice
leaned over and touched Matt's shoulder. "We don't have to
hate each other all the time," she said.

He shrugged off her hand, propped himself on his
elbows and looked straight at her. "You want to take everything now, Alice. Every fucking thing that ever meant anything
to me—my home, my child. The woman I loved."

"Christ, Matt, *I* am the woman you loved. Stop talking
about me like I'm somebody else."

He met her eyes. "You *are* somebody else."

"Jesus," she said, looking away. "Who are *you*, then?"
She looked back, chewing her lip. "I'm just asking for your
help, Matt."

"Hire somebody."

"There's no money."

"You've gone through five thousand dollars?"

"Come on, Matt. You're always so damn critical."
She stood up suddenly; he had to roll onto his side to keep her
in view. "You know, you never help anymore." Alice folded
her arms over her chest. "You never help with Christopher
now. You haven't once helped me with my kennel." She
walked a few steps away and stood at the edge of the water for
a minute, watching it flow past, slowly grinding her heel. Matt
watched the muscles flex in her long tanned leg. Turning
around, she said softly, "Look. I don't ask much from you
anymore. I certainly don't like to ask for your help." She came
back to him, knelt and put her fingertips on his chest. "It's hard

to ask for your help," she said, tapping her fingers against his sternum. "You always want something in return."

Her touch was so obvious it made him smile, but only fleetingly. "Why bother with the roof if you can't finish the rest of it?" he asked, raising his hand to brush her fingers away. But her fingernails were light and hard on his skin now, drawing long multiple spirals that caused his stomach muscles to go flat and hard. He let his hand drop back to his side.

"Jake said I can owe him the money."

"Then why don't you have *him* do the roof?"

"Because he still has to put in the doors and windows. He needs to close it to the weather." She hooked a fingertip under his belt. "He's already working twice as hard as anybody else. Why can't *you* help me?" She ran her finger under the waistband of his jeans.

"This is so blatant, Alice. Aren't you embarrassed?"

"We're past embarrassment," she said. "Promise you'll help." But she looked embarrassed a moment later, when she spotted Tom Edwards coming up the path from the road. Her face was curious to watch readjusting—a quick sequence of expressions tried on and discarded.

"Howdy, folks," Tom said, when he got close. "Mind if I join you?"

Alice's teeth gleamed white. "Have a seat."

Matt frowned. He couldn't get used to anyone saying "Howdy" in Vermont, especially when they came from Connecticut. Tom was *Jake's* friend anyhow, not his—always showing up uninvited.

Tom put his hands in his pockets and looked at his feet. He dug one sneaker into the grass, pushing out the little plants. "It sure is a real pretty morning. How're *you* doing, Matt?"

"Just great, Tom. Sit down. Stop pawing up the grass like a bull."

"Sorry." He looked from side to side and then settled himself, wincing elaborately.

Matt asked, "How are the house plans coming?"

"I just keep making it smaller. Everything's too expensive." He shook his head and winced again. "I used up all my money buying land with Jake."

"Buying land is just getting your foot in the door," said Matt.

"How *are* things going at Jake's?" Alice asked.

"They're okay. I feel like I'm in the way, though." He pulled a little stone out of the grass and rolled it between his fingers. "*His* house isn't very big, either. And now that they've got Megan as well as Brittany." He flipped the stone into the water. "Jake wasn't even married when I enlisted."

Alice got up. "A lot happens in four years, Tom." She smoothed down her shorts. Bending over Christopher she stroked the fine hair away from his eyes, then said, "I'll get us some coffee."

Tom lay back carefully on the grass, adjusting his spine. He was silent for a moment, watching an oriole in the crown of the birch overhead, the slender branches bending beneath the bird's weight. They heard the screen door open and close, and Tom said, "You're lucky to have a woman." Matt ground his teeth. After a minute he said, "I have a woman, too. Marilyn. She's still out west."

"Is she coming to Vermont?"

"She's got a little boy. And I don't even have the money to fly them here."

Matt glanced over at him and shook his head.

"I sure do miss her. Five hundred dollars for tickets, though." Tom shifted on the ground and grimaced suddenly, his neck oddly bent. He tried to reach his shoulder blade but couldn't, and looking sideways he said, "Matt. Would you rub my neck? I woke up this morning and I couldn't even turn my head."

Matt paused, then said, "Well, sure, I guess so. Where does it hurt?"

Tom bent forward and pointed. "Right here."

Matt felt awkward touching him. As his fingers kneaded the tan flesh, Tom flinched repeatedly, saying, "Oh, yes, right there." It felt weird to rub his body, his khaki T-shirt dirty, his back thin, almost scrawny. Tom was just about moaning with relief or pleasure and Matt wondered how he could ever have been a marine. Matt looked across at Christopher and thought of the feel of *his* body—all soft and new, constant growth and almost no history. When Alice came back she looked amused. Matt hadn't seen her smile for days; now it seemed she couldn't stop. It disconcerted Matt so much that *he* stopped, though. "Don't stop," Tom said out loud, and rolled his head gingerly from side to side.

Matt thought it would be like this for him to be alone—soliciting whatever human touch he could, from people who were essentially strangers. His body felt handsome and chilled and the world seemed wasteful. He looked up at Alice. In the light glinting up from the water she looked hard and sharp—with her thin nose and stern eyes, she had a classic beauty, a cold elegance.

He remembered *her* human touch, the serenity that once came with waking to the pressure of her body against his chest and legs, rolling over and making love, still half–asleep. Just warmly giving and taking, bodies without mind or name. Just loving—a glowing, safe, uncomplicated thing.

When Tom finally left, Alice sat close to Matt and said, "I don't really like Tom. He doesn't do anything except..." she searched for words, "not drink."

Matt shrugged. "That's a lot for him, I think. He's probably okay, Alice. He's lonely."

"You just like *anybody*."

"I never said I *liked* him."

She leaned against Matt, put her hand on his leg and slowly skimmed her fingers up and down from his hip to his knee. "We can still help each other." After a moment she took his hand and put it on the inside of her thigh, just under the cuff of her shorts. Her skin was smooth, with fine blond hairs, and

167

her flesh was soft. Matt closed his eyes. It was amazing how little he really understood things—Alice, himself, love, sex. Less and less each day. She moved her leg slightly and he slid his fingers under the cuff of her shorts, his fingertips under the edge of her panties. He was surprised how little resistance there was—she was already moist and his fingertips slipped just inside her. Sex with her now always made him think of Christopher. "We can still love each other," she said. Matt kept his eyes closed. The new grass tickled his rib cage. "Promise," she said.

Promises. Matt stood on the roof with a long-handled mop; he spread a wide band of black shiny tar onto the raw wood and the top half of the last course of roofing. He carefully unrolled the next section of roofing onto the tar, slid the big piece down to the chalk line, evened it up, then nailed the top half thoroughly. It was so hot. He thought of all the roofs he'd covered on this place. It always seemed to be the hottest days of the summer that he was up there in the sun, rolling out tar and sweat, rolling out white double coverage rolled roofing. It seemed so stupid now.

He pounded nails by the score. Each blow of the hammer echoed back to him from across the brook. He wondered why he was doing all this. She'd never get to use the kennel anyway—they'd lose the whole place when they split up. They were just automatons now, mindlessly following some obsolete agenda, yesterday's schedule, orders from nowhere. His knees ached.

Matt stood up on the roof and stretched. The sudden change in posture made him dizzy and he closed his eyes. Every place he'd ever lived was really somebody else's. For a dozen years he'd dreamed of having his own. Build a home and raise up a family. Keep pigs and sheep and chickens. Grow a garden, plant an orchard, heat with wood. Last summer he had sheep on the place for the first time, and pigs for the second. The orchard was three years old now and Matt was twenty-six.

Alice was building her kennel near the place they called Christopher's Cradle, where the main brook curved toward the road for a moment before flowing away again. That spot was as close as they could drive to the house site. When Matt worked clearing the land two years ago they used to keep Christopher's cradle there next to the parked truck, in the warm shade by the water. As Matt built the house, they kept his crib there, and then his playpen.

High above Matt the sky was blue and open, and a wind came in from the west, promising change. Heat shimmered up from the white surface of the roofing he had already installed, and the white gravel in the black felt was brilliant in the sun at close range. Matt squinted as he looked across it to their house on the far side of the brook. Christopher and Alice were inside, he supposed. For once her dogs lay asleep in their runs by the house. Matt wondered if someday "Christopher's Cradle" might become a place name, a name on a map, and cause people to stop and think about its origin, long after he and Alice had gone their separate ways and this kennel had been reduced to forest mold. He listened to the quiet, the strange silence of the dogs, the brook and the wind.

Yesterday's sex with Alice had left him feeling more like a casual stranger than ever. It made him remember her shower last week. Matt had been reading on the deck when she walked out, naked, almost contemptuous of his presence, to wash under the solar shower hung by the greenhouse door. She arched her blond body under the delicate spray of water, soaped her breasts and armpits, and turned, flexing, to rinse her body off. Turning back, she caught Matt watching her; she tossed her hair out of her eyes and stared at him until he looked away.

Matt was about a third of the way up the kennel roof when the dogs started, their loud mindless noise crude and incessant, shattering the background of birdsong and brook. He looked down and saw Tom Edwards come slowly along the road, kicking little stones out of his way. A man alone, barely making it. He would be down there himself soon enough, Matt thought. So much for promises.

Matt waved. Tom's pace didn't falter, and Matt studied him critically, like looking into a mirror. Tom had told him yesterday he should spend more time with Alice. That felt ludicrous, getting advice from Tom Edwards, with his stories of marine buddies, hung over and sick every morning—a bunch of losers. Tom went to AA meetings almost every night here—that's how he spent *his* time. Matt just couldn't believe that somewhere out west there was a woman for Tom, waiting for him, waiting for his call.

He shook his head slowly. From the rooftop he looked west but he couldn't seem to focus beyond his house. He thought of Alice, and their lovemaking the day before, burying his face in the bowl of her pelvis, piquant smell of woman and sex spread over the softness of her belly, downy blond hair and tiny wrinkles, cheek against skin. He wanted to rest his face there forever. She pushed him off though; she said his head weighed too much.

Tom reached the kennel and stood in the driveway, rolling his neck and studying his feet. Alice's kuvaszok barked relentlessly, goading each other on, raucous and inexorable. Tom looked thin and small on the ground, and Matt came down the ladder to shake his hand, asking, "How's your neck doing?"

Tom's free hand massaged his shoulder. "Okay, I guess." He looked around Matt as the big dogs came pounding down the bank and tore across the main brook, splashing muddy water everywhere, cascades of dull droplets flat in the sun. Moments later Alice crossed on the footbridge, two-by-six planks on log stringers, high above the stream. She studied the roof as she came. Four courses of the white asphalted felt were in place. At least ten more would be necessary to finish the west side. She shook her head and turned judiciously to Tom. "Slow but sure. How do you like my kennel?"

"Roof looks good, Alice." Tom absentmindedly scratched one of the dogs behind her ears. "Yup, the whole place looks very nice." He squatted down and the big kuvasz pushed her nose into Tom's dirty khaki T-shirt and sneezed. Tom rubbed the top of her head hard.

Matt asked, "Christopher slept through all that?"

"Um-hmm."

Tom looked at the ground, then up at Matt. "Well, I called Marilyn again last night."

"Who's Marilyn?" Alice asked.

"My woman in San Diego."

She smiled at him. "I didn't know you had a woman, Tom. How's she doing?"

"Okay, I guess. She's lost her job, though. I've talked to her every night now for the last week. One thing and then another keeps her from coming, and now her money's run out. I'd send her the money myself if I could."

"Why don't you borrow some from Jake?" asked Alice.

"Jake! He's always complaining about how he doesn't have any money." Tom turned his head and spat. "The people who complain the loudest are the ones who have the most. That's what I've noticed. Marriage sure has changed him."

"Jake and everybody else," Matt said.

Alice frowned. "Babies change things," she said evenly.

"Well, I just don't know what to do next."

"Go to a bank," Alice said.

"They're worse than Jake. I can't even get a construction loan." Tom massaged the dog's big head.

Alice said, "Marilyn can find money somewhere. People can always find money if it's important enough."

"Not women, though."

"Especially women, Tom."

Tom looked at her, then at Matt. "I've been thinking of going back, but I don't know what good it would do." His hands grew still in the dog's coat, the coarse white hair gradually unwinding from his stained fingers.

"There's always some way to make it work." Alice stood back and looked up at the kennel building. "The roof looks great, Matt."

"I've been looking for a job, but there's nothing around," Tom said.

"Tell me about it. I've been looking for three years," Alice said.

Tom nodded solemnly. Suddenly the dog shook herself and water flew everywhere. Alice grinned at Tom ducking. Matt sighed. He thought of all the things that might never happen because of five hundred dollars for airplane tickets. He looked at Alice. The slow saturation of loneliness.

In his mind he saw a composite of all the women he'd loved, and wanted to love, but in the quick flash of his vision it wasn't an image he saw, but motion—swinging hair across a shoulder, hips moving under fabric, breasts shifting under a wool sweater. He felt arms reach out and draw him in, he felt his head cradled there among the smell of wool and hair and woman's scent and sweat. Almost to himself he said, "I'll lend you the money."

Alice put her hands on her hips. "And where are we going to come up with five hundred dollars?"

"Hell, I don't know. Somewhere."

"We don't *have* any extra money, Matt."

"You can always find money if it's important enough."

"Well, this kennel's pretty important," she said, biting each word. "Let me know how much you find."

Matt frowned. He swept his arm in an impatient gesture that took in the whole project. "None of this stuff means anything, Alice."

"None of this *means* anything?"

"Not compared to people," he tried to explain.

But Alice just shook her head slowly, clenching her teeth.

"We're not building a home here anymore," Matt said. "This is just a place for dogs now. This is a dog house."

"This is my *kennel*, Matt," Alice said, stepping forward.

Matt stiffened but Tom stood up then and said, "Now I didn't intend that. I didn't intend to cause an argument here."

He looked at Alice. "I don't want a loan from you folks. I'll work everything out somehow." At first Matt thought he was just responding to Alice's anger, then he heard the insistence in Tom's voice—it wasn't just money that was lacking, something else was wrong. This was all just talk. He glanced at Alice, but she was staring into the distance now. Matt studied her face—her lips drawn back, her nose sharp and hard. She was almost sneering. He shivered. Yesterday they had lain together like vampires, bloodsuckers, full of wanton desire. She had said afterwards, *That was easy, wasn't it?* her smile perfect teeth without soul.

"Yup," Tom said, backing up a couple of steps. "You don't need to worry. I'll work it out myself. But thanks very much all the same." He scuffed his foot in the dirt. "I sure didn't mean to bother you folks. I was just passing through." He turned and began to walk toward the road. "I'll see you all later. You have a nice day now."

Alice watched him shuffle out of earshot. "I can imagine what she's like," she said, rolling her eyes.

"So can I," said Matt, turning away from her. He had a sudden, sinking picture of a hard worn woman sucking a cigarette, eyes squinting from the smoke, laughing at some barroom joke, long yellow teeth with lots of gum showing. He wrapped his arms across his chest.

"What would they *do* here, anyhow?" asked Alice. "Go to AA meetings all the time?"

Matt watched Tom reach the road, then hesitate a moment before he started toward Jake's. He said, "You know, there probably isn't any woman out west." There was no answer from behind him, though. He turned around. "Maybe there never was."

But Alice remained silent, just staring. Finally she said, "Christ. Then why did you offer him five hundred dollars?" She shook her head impatiently. "I'll never under-stand you," she said, glaring now, swallowing hard. Then she spun on her heel and stalked away. Her dogs followed silently, their tails low. Matt watched her cross the bridge and stamp up the path to the house. She never looked back. After a while he tightened his nail apron and climbed up onto the kennel roof.

A woman in the west. Once she had been like that—a promise beautiful in the distance, hope all coiled up like folded time. A waxing light expanding toward him, flooding life with brilliance, lifting him into luminosity.

He glanced down and frowned—Tom Edwards could just be seen in the distance, a small figure paused in the roadway, looking from left to right. A woman in the west. How could that ever be a real thing? Marilyn was real for Tom only as long as he didn't try to bring her here—the moment he did, she'd cease to exist entirely. Some western mirage.

Matt shook his head. There are no saviors on silver planes. Greasy metal machines that scream. If she came at all she'd come out of the sun, a dark fleck in the radiance, growing larger and larger and larger.

Standing there on the plywood sheathing, Matt wished he could just live among the leafy branches in the summer sky, stay up there for good—high above the roads and paths, the comings and goings, the people and their problems and their dreams. He wanted to remain up there forever in the sunlight and breeze, the green light and yellow wood—let the world below swirl by without him from now on.

The house door slammed suddenly, cutting off his thoughts, and suddenly Alice's dogs began to bark again. And then there was Alice herself, striding down the path triumphantly, moving fast, waving a thick sheaf of papers in her hand. But Matt had already pulled the ladder onto the roof, and now he started to climb up toward the ridge.

CHAPTER 17

Cæsura

Matt

Maybe there was a limit to loss after all—halfway up
the cliff face I'd slipped for the second time and almost fallen.
That whole majestic thing just rotten rock—fractures you
couldn't see and handholds you couldn't trust. Maybe I'd take
those lines to my death, chant them through eternity.
> But I'm his **father.**
> That's not enough.
> He's my **son.**
> That's not enough.

All through the mountains those lines had repeated,
rhythmic as tires on pavement. At the top of the last pass
through the eastern escarpment I'd quit driving, weary of the
incessant refrain. I parked my truck at the pullout for back-
packers, and started on foot to the height of the precipice. But
the lines remained in my head; they began to pound in my neck,
one with my pulse, one with my breath, banging and heaving
by the time I pulled myself up over the cresting lip of shattered
stone. I crawled across the grassy verge to the edge of the trees
and settled back against the biggest trunk I could find, thick
roots firmly planted, reaching deep. Family and home and this
sickness in my heart.

So add Christopher to the list, make it a trinity, gone as
fast as fire. Home and child and the woman I loved.

From the top of the cliff, cloud shadows slid smoothly
over low mountains, slippery as the passage of time. Gliding
east and south, undulating over foothills and lowlands until
they flattened out with the country itself, stretching away

toward the distant sea—toward Boston, that city of earliest
dreams, beginning and end of things, and Leslie of course, lost
somewhere in those ruins, stretching away, Leslie, slipping
backward in time. So many times I'd sworn I would never go
back. Now I didn't know if I was running from loss or returning to it.

From the top of that cliff I could slide smoothly into
my past, roll down that eastern escarpment, slip into those days
with Leslie, into that city of broken dreams. And part of me
wanted to, locked into loss, a prisoner of time. This eternal
attempt at redemption. But it was too late for that now—I'd
accumulated ghosts, layers and layers of loss, and you can only
deal with one layer at a time. It was my recent past I had to
contain, Alice and Christopher, my home in Vermont. Because
I think there probably are limits to everything, including the
chances we're given to start over.

In my life I have loved three women, and all of them
seemed to converge on that sun-drenched rock, violating space
and time. It was Sarah now I was traveling to see, Sarah for
hope and understanding, for the only love I hadn't lost. Sarah
who had helped me survive the time before this one.

And Michael, of course, my best friend during those
six years in Boston. He found Sarah and fell in love with her
my last summer there, although by then I was doing everything
I could to escape that city, that void in my life, that space that
was Leslie.

It was Sarah who finally persuaded me to go home to
Vermont, to climb out of the hole, to start over again. Sarah
from Boston. But I met her in mountains—in northern New
Hampshire, lichen and granite and sunlight splashed all over
the Franconias. Stretched out after lunch on the summit of Mt.
Lafayette, our packs propped against rocks as back rests, I
pointed out a solitary hawk soaring in a thermal updraft. "I'm
tired," Michael said, as I reached around for my camera. "I
don't care about any hawks." He'd carried Sarah's pack more
than half the way up the mountain—the two packs together

weighed almost eighty pounds. "This is a lot of grunt work, you know, Matt." He shifted slightly against the five-inch back bands and pulled his dark felt hat low over his eyes. Sarah got up, though, and moved about fifteen yards away to a better vantage point. She stood silhouetted against the sky, looking out over the long Franconia valley, her hands on her hips, strong chin raised and long black hair blowing back from her consummate face like a banner. Michael watched her from under the brim of his hat. "Matt, old man, someday soon I'm going to marry that woman." Then he rose and joined her. Their arms went around each other's waists and their dark shapes merged together. I took their picture first, then the hawk's.

Together we made a dozen trips that summer—leaving Boston behind for the northern birch forests, climbing up through sun-dappled greenery and whiteness to the more rugged stands of pungent fir, with their smell of altitude and wind, climbing until finally we were above even the highest firs, those dwarfed and shrunken trees at timberline, climbing out onto rocky peaks of blasted granite, the earth laid out below us in much the same way as now, but closer then, somehow. Everything was.

For a moment I felt flooded with the intensity of that summer—the mountain tops littered with broken boulders, sunshine washing Sarah's darkly muscled legs, the movement of her buttocks as she hiked in front of me, thin crescents of untanned flesh at the edge of fabric. Everything so vital then. Sarah's rolling hips wide and broad, a cradle designed for bearing children. I made up songs in my head about loving her. Sometimes I hummed them aloud.

I lay down now on the cliff top's grassy verge and closed my eyes and thought about our final trip that summer— the Mt. Washington trip—the one where Sarah threw away Michael's Icelandic sweater. We'd finished that climb without trouble, four days in the mountains, and Michael waited by the trailhead with the three heavy packs while Sarah and I drove her Volkswagen back to the starting point for my car. About halfway there, where the road cut high up on a steep hillside, Sarah abruptly pulled over onto the shoulder. "Let's see the mountains we did," she said, slapping my thigh the hearty way a man would. She jumped out. The wind blew cold up from the notch, and Sarah stood close to me next to the car. I put my arm around her shoulders. She looked sideways and said, "Could you get me a sweater?" I went around to the front of the Volkswagen and opened the lid. A worn grayish one lay folded beside the spare tire in the musty trunk. When I brought it to Sarah she looked at it with disgust. Saying, "God, not that one!" she took it with both hands, mashed it into a ball, and flung it over the guardrail. She threw it out hard, as far as she could, over the rusty cables into the gorge.

"Sarah," I said. "That was Michael's favorite."

"Yeah. Well, you don't know the story behind it, Matt."

"I *do* know that story," I said. I knew all of Michael's stories, especially the sea stories. Michael had given up the sea, as he put it, in order to marry Sarah. At twenty-four, he'd been an able-bodied seaman for six years. "A quarter of my life," he used to say. The sweater came from his first voyage, the one that took him to Iceland. He'd described Iceland as moon-like, a barren land—all lava flows, no trees anywhere, not even roads outside the villages. His ship stayed in port for eleven days, and during that time Michael fell in love with a fisherman's daughter. A long, stunning girl—I've seen the photographs. Her whole family wanted him to stay and marry her. He almost did. Toward the end he moved into their stone house by the sea. The young American. Sailing from Woods Hole to Reykjavik, never to come home again. The girl knit a sweater for him; she finished it the day he left, and for years afterwards he wore it constantly, even after he met Sarah.

Sarah stood with her hands on her hips, looking at Mt. Washington. "Well, then," she said, "you understand how important it is not to tell Michael." She shivered violently.

178

"Damn it, Matt. I've had it up to here with his women." Then she put her arms around my waist and I held her in the cold sunshine, the smell of evergreen. She pressed herself hard against me, making solid contact all along the lengths of our bodies, like a cat, sinuous, a gentle undulating curve. I kissed her—I couldn't help it.

But she pushed her hands against my chest. "No," she murmured, "No," she said, and I took a long deep breath as she pulled away. A logging truck roared by and in the rush of following wind and diesel smoke I thought I heard, "I wish we could."

I looked at Sarah. She shook her head. I looked over the guardrail. The sweater hadn't gone far; thick and bulky, it lodged on a few stubby hemlocks just out of sight of the highway. It might have been the gray corpse of some animal struck by a car. I could have climbed down and retrieved it, but in the end I decided not to.

The beautiful Sarah. Four years later I could still feel her embrace, that impossible welcome, urging me home.

Wherever that was. If such a place existed at all. Vermont to Boston to Vermont to Boston—I was just closing circles, repeating cycles, defining home by the places it wasn't. Four years later I was back where I'd started, back where I'd finished, sideslipping, freefalling, spinning out of control. Circles to cycles to spirals descending. Leslie and Alice and Sarah.

Sarah. And then on her porch, in the shelter of a home not broken by divorce, a moment of grace. Caught for an instant in Sarah's arms, the free fall checked, her embrace a reprieve, her love without question. One constant thing left in the whole shifting world.

I didn't meet Patricia until I went inside. She seemed beautiful, too, although I couldn't understand why—perhaps it was her attitude, or maybe her enthusiasm. Probably it was just me—where I was in time. She looked almost like a boy, with her short dark hair and small breasts. She wore loose blue

jeans, one of Michael's hats, and a man's Oxford shirt, stiff
with gesso. She had a quick laugh, flashing eyes, a diamond in
her nose. I don't understand why a woman would put a
diamond in her nose.

Patricia and Sarah drank wine at the table against the
window, the kitchen around them all thick white-painted
woodwork and cut-glass knobs, chopping blocks and old
wooden cabinets. And Benjamin a peripheral blur, showing me
things he had made—crayon drawings and paintings, and clay
sculptures with colored wooden sticks that made me think of
scrap insulation board, soft foam two inches thick, covered
with foil and bristling like porcupines with the 16-common
nails Christopher had pounded in one afternoon with his plastic
club of a hammer. And I remembered the crayon drawings
he'd made all over the pantry walls the day I was reglazing the
window in that filthy room. And the paintings we'd made that
first day in the old house, now encircling the upper walls of the
dreary kitchen like a bright living frieze, a halo, a rising light.

But you can't just take him out of my life.

You'll get to see him every other weekend.

*I have the right to see him every **day**. He's my **son**.*

That's not enough.

With a clinking of metal Patricia helped Sarah as-
semble a new pasta machine; Benjamin had ruined her old one
extruding green modeling clay. "This isn't as good as my first
one," Sarah said, turning the machine over in her hands.
"These new ones are so glitzy—no substance to them."

Late light came low past the flowers on the windowsill
and glinted bright and hard off the plated metal, attracting
Benjamin's attention. "*I'll* take it," he said.

"No, Ben. You have my first one."

"But that one's old."

"Right, kid." She gave him a hug. "You're beginning
to sound like your father."

Michael was in the pantry unable to find Irish whiskey—I could hear him shouting something to Sarah. He found

180

a bottle of Bombay gin and brought it to the table with a shot glass. He offered it first to Patricia, who said she'd never had any before. She held the bottle under her nose, grimaced and said, "It smells like the next day."

Sarah smiled slightly. I also declined, and Michael drank off two shots. "So how *are* you, Sarah?" I asked. She looked wonderful. She had limitless dark eyes and I'd forgotten that if I gazed right into them when I spoke to her, I lost my place.

"Life goes on. Nothing really changes. How are *you* doing, Matt? *That's* the question."

"Well, it's all over now. We've moved into separate places. The house is up for sale. Along with that stupid kennel."

"Where are you living?"

"A rented ruin. It doesn't even have glass in the windows. The first thing I do when I come home from work is chase the birds out."

She looked at me questioningly. "It's almost winter, Matt."

"I know, I know. I'm working on it."

"But why?"

"Money. And the views are nice."

She narrowed her eyes the way lawyers do. "The views?"

"The only other places I could afford were these dark little camps, deep in the woods in the middle of nowhere. You'd go inside, there'd be three or four dingy rooms in a row, and in the one furthest back, in the light from a television, there'd be this mossy armchair with a fungus growing out of it, drinking beer. I *need* the views, Sarah."

"It's good to see you again, Matt," Sarah said, smiling and giving me a hug. "But really, are you okay?"

"Really, I don't know what the hardest part is anymore."

"What about Alice?"

"She's like a totally different person now."

"Christopher?"

"I get to see him every other weekend."

Sarah took my hand.

"Every other weekend, Sarah."

"That can be enough," she said, squeezing my hand. "You'll see. You'll always be his father, Matt. Lots of fathers are with their kids every day, but they're never really with their kids at all." She looked me over closely. "It sure is good to see you."

Across the kitchen, Michael burst out laughing at something Patricia said. He still had that tremendous magnetism—his wild eyes and wild hair, face unshaven, his great big teeth and sexual smile. He joked with Patricia about being secretly Cuban. She kept touching him as he talked.

Patricia was twenty-one. In September she'd moved into the apartment below Michael's new studio. She'd come from Ireland to study at the Museum School; Michael was a brand-new instructor there. Her voice suddenly rose, carrying clearly across the room: "I was lonely and new. I thought that would set me apart. But the only thing that makes me different here is my accent."

Michael said, "Loneliness is part of the human condition. You'll never change that." He sat down beside her and put his arm around her shoulders and gave her a hug. "Come on, Patricia."

"Oh yes I will. I'll not be lonely *my* whole life." She shrugged her shoulders, shaking off Michael's arm, stood up and pushed her forefinger into his chest. "Loneliness is an American condition. An American male tradition."

Michael snorted. "Now don't get personal, Patricia."

"I've seen it a hundred times already. You love it."

"Loneliness is the basis for art," he said.

Loneliness is a creeping beast. Over the last two years the loneliness in our Vermont house had grown until it became a tangible thing. It seemed impossible there could be room for

it, with Alice complaining and Christopher crying and all her
dogs barking, but there it was—waiting for my return at the end
of each day, finally driving me out. I'd stay away as much as I
could, and when I did come home, I'd work outside, or wander
through the woods and fields until evening became dark night.

Michael followed Patricia out into the dining room and
in the space they left I could feel loneliness shuffling around,
sniffing in corners, looking for a place to settle down. The
stinking beast. I wondered if Michael had ever been lonely,
and glanced at Sarah. She felt my gaze and rose. She offered
me a glass of wine and I took it, smiling back at her ambiguous
face. Her fingers lingered on my wrist.

Sarah gave Benjamin an early dinner and I sat down
with them. When I asked how he liked preschool, he said it
was okay—he liked his teacher a lot, and his new friends. He
liked to paint. But it was a lot harder than his other school, he
said, and besides, he missed the sandbox there. Sarah laughed,
and I did, too. Our eyes locked; I knew how close they had
always been.

Christopher would miss water, that was his element of
obsession. Puddles and streams, pots and pans, drinking straws
that bent into fancy curlicues that he couldn't make work, tubs
and faucets, the toilet that rocked on the rotted floor.

I want joint custody, at least.
You don't have a chance.
*But I'm his **father**.*
That's not enough.

Sarah said in some ways she felt sorry to see Benjamin
grow up; a lot more time existed in her life now. "I feel like
five years ago I stopped everything, and now I don't know how
to start again." She poured Benjamin more apple juice. I
pushed up my sleeves and started to wash some dishes. "Like
my career as a buyer—you remember the women's store. I was
about to become a partner there." She brought over Benjamin's
plate and silverware. "And my poetry—I miss that tremen-
dously. I'd just begun to publish some pieces." She cleaned

Benjamin's face and hung the washcloth next to the sink. "Enjoying my marriage." She paused and looked straight at me. "Being in love." She sighed, the lightest breath, then turned and said, "Come on, Ben, say 'Good night.' It's time to go to bed."

I stayed in the kitchen by myself for a while, appreciating the familiarity of things, touching objects I hadn't felt for years, feeling a connection I once took for granted. Coming back to Boston made me want to start over again, pick up where I'd left off four years ago. But how many chances are we given?

I wandered through the downstairs, looking for Michael, and eventually found him outside on the porch, drinking wine and smoking a cigarette. He stood with one foot hiked up on the railing, staring off into space, like he was looking out to sea. Patricia was nowhere in sight. I raised my glass silently and stood next to him, watching the rain begin to collect on the pavement below. Like most houses in the Back Bay, his was built a century ago, set close to the brick sidewalk and raised half a story above the street level. As the rain increased he turned to me and began to talk about his students.

"I'm in love with them all. They're all so...unformed. Everything is possible with them. For them. It's all wide open." He leaned on the railing and took a long drag of his cigarette, squinting into the distance. "It's like...well, there are times in a life where anything can happen. I'm at a time like that now. So are you, for that matter." He turned around and studied me. "They're the best times of all, Matt. You just haven't appreciated that yet."

Michael started to pace back and forth across the porch. "Benjamin's almost five, and he's pretty well set for a while—his life and his school are all laid out. Sarah will be okay—I've been working like crazy these last five years—I've done hundreds, thousands of illustrations by now." He stopped and stood in front of me. "Soon I'll be *thirty*." He took another long draw on his cigarette, then blew the smoke out slowly.

"At thirty, the best part of your life is behind you." He started pacing again. "You meet your responsibilities, then you go on. But for a little while there, before you *do* go on, you're free—you're in an interspace—you can go anywhere. The kids I teach are like that; they're in an interspace, too. That's why I love them."

"What about your kids at BU?" I asked. " How did they fit in?" Michael had walked out of his classroom one afternoon without any explanation to anyone; he'd gone to Mexico, where he stayed for a couple of months. Sarah said she'd gotten one phone call from him before he left the country—the only call he'd made.

"That's no different," he said. "I was as desperate as those kids were. They all understood. They were the only ones who did." He laughed. "It's true BU would never hire me again. I was surprised the Museum School did. But I don't care."

He went on. "What I can't stand is dead time. Sarah gets annoyed when I take girls for rides on my motorcycle. But she won't come herself. She wants me to be at home with her, but she doesn't want anything to do with me. Just be there, around her, doing nothing, put on hold, dead time. I hate it. The dead time. I don't feel as if I *have* plenty of time. I rode up to the Cape last weekend with Patricia. It was a beautiful day. We didn't do anything, just rode up and rode back. It was great."

About a year ago, when my own marriage was already coming undone, Michael telephoned several times to talk about fidelity, his troubled sense of approaching thirty, his sudden solicitation by young women—one gave him a wedding commission and an invitation to sleep with her before she married; another, like Patricia, had a studio below his, and she'd come up in the evenings as he worked on his oil paintings. Michael wanted everything: his youth, those women, his fidelity to Sarah. It distressed him so much he talked to Sarah about it. She told him, "If you have an affair with some girl I *never* want to know about it." He never came to any resolution those nights he called, and I'd never asked him what he chose.

Once, after Michael had to get an HIV test because a dental hygienist cut herself treating him, he said his biggest concern wasn't death but infidelity. He'd remained faithful to Sarah throughout their marriage, and he felt the only way he could contract the virus would be from her, and that evidence of her infidelity was what he feared most of all. His results came back negative.

"So, are you and Patricia lovers now?" I asked.

"No. I've never been unfaithful to Sarah. But that's not something you take for granted. Every minute you start over."

"Of course, but what does being faithful mean?" You want to sing this song with me? "How did *Sarah* get to spend last weekend?"

"Probably doing something with Benjamin. You can't be together all the time. We just spent two weeks together in Jamaica."

Sarah made shellfish for dinner, with pasta, and pesto from basil she grew herself. She sat next to me at the table, talking about Benjamin's school. "So I'm able to work there almost full time as an aide. Unofficially—I'm not really trained for it. But I love doing it."

"That sounds great. And lucky."

"You make the luck happen, Matt." She paused for a moment, touching my forearm, examining my face. "You know what I mean? Make the best of the time you've got."

"Every other weekend?"

"If that's all there is."

"Is that enough?"

"If that's all there is," she repeated. I frowned, swallowing a mouthful of quahogs. "You do what you can," Sarah said, placing the platter of shell fish in front of me. "What choice have we got?" We ate silently for a minute, then she changed the subject. "I've been trying to write poems again."

Patricia burst out laughing over something Michael said. Sarah looked up.

"It hasn't been easy," she said.

Michael choked on his wine, sputtering a little. I caught his eye, but he didn't say anything. Patricia looked down at her plate. Sarah exhaled, studying Michael. She poured me some more wine.

"Benjamin's been a real help. He doesn't mind playing by himself while I write."

"And drink wine," said Michael. He leaned over the table toward me. "She's half loaded when I come home at night."

"*When* you come home at night."

I passed the bread around. Michael tipped over his wine glass reaching for it, and Patricia jumped up before anyone else to get a sponge and towel.

Michael gestured to me and I passed the wine bottle to him. "You're getting drunk," I said.

"Not me."

I took some more salad and turned back to my plate. For a long time Sarah remained silent. "I feel so alone sometimes," she said finally. I touched her arm.

Michael sat back in his chair, gesturing with both hands, saying something to Patricia about negative space.

"And I feel so old now."

"Sarah, you're still in your twenties. You're a beautiful woman." I leaned over and kissed her on her cheek, but she continued to watch Michael.

Michael was telling an old sea story to Patricia—the last time he worked as a seaman, on the URI research vessel. The ship put into Halifax and he stood in a phone booth outside a bar when several drunken fishermen came by and decided to tip the booth over and beat him up. As they shouted in Portuguese and rocked the booth, Michael held up the receiver and pointed at it with his other hand and said, "Mama. Mama."

They laughed then, saying "Mama," themselves, and went on their way. It was Sarah he was really calling, but he didn't tell Patricia that. An old story indeed—he hadn't known Sarah long then.

I felt Sarah's hand close over mine, and heard her say, "It's like I'm not even here."

When dinner ended we sat around the table, and I tried to exclude Patricia and see just the two of them—Michael and Sarah—as a couple, but I couldn't. With her long fingers on his arm, her broad soft voice in his ear, and her bright smile filling his eyes, Patricia was separating Michael. A different couple was emerging instead, new, and glitzy somehow, bright and hard and smelling of emptiness.

Then Patricia stood up and thanked Sarah for dinner, apologized and said she had to go. She went to the closet to get her jacket. Michael said he had to return to his studio to finish some work, and he'd see her out.

Sarah said, "You don't have to go back to your studio again tonight."

Michael stopped halfway across the room. "I have a deadline on this work, Sarah. You never appreciate that. This stuff has to go out by tomorrow morning."

"Matt just got here."

Michael came over to my chair. "Matt, old man. I'll see you later on. Sarah will take care of you until I get back. Sorry I couldn't get this stuff done sooner."

Patricia and Michael went outside, and Sarah went into the kitchen. I went out to the porch to have a cigarette. It had stopped raining during dinner; the sidewalks now glistened, water puddled on saturated brick, slowly draining away. My memories of Boston were always of misty street lamps, light reflecting from wet brick, brick walks cast into ripples over the years by tree roots growing underneath.

A sound of rhythmic tapping came up from the sidewalk below me. Michael and Patricia were skipping in place, side by side, their arms around each other's waists. No sound but the tap, tap, tap, and then Patricia's laughter.

Watching them, I thought again of the first time I met Sarah. At the base of Mt. Lafayette there lay an abandoned field not far from the trailhead. It's probably grown up to brush now. I remembered Sarah and Michael walking in that meadow under the mountain, walking with their arms around each other's waists, down the gentle slope among tall grass. Grass like the sea, wind rippling waves. Sarah looked like she was leading him out of the water. It made me sad somehow, wondering how things would turn out. I still have the walking stick I cut from the edge of that meadow.

I heard the porch door open and close, and I felt Sarah come up beside me in the darkness. Then I felt her arm around my own waist, her hip against my side, the warmth of her body penetrating the cloth on my leg. I thought I heard a sob; I put my arm around her shoulders and turned toward her. She pushed her face into my shirt, and I embraced her with both arms. After a moment I realized she wasn't crying, though, and I held her away from me a little to study her face. Her eyes were dry and impossible to read and I thought of Michael then—I wanted him to come home. I wanted all of us to come home.

Sarah shook her head and her long hair rippled. "Poor Patricia—she's so young. She's like a drop of water in a river but she doesn't know it yet. And Michael—it's like he's trying to hold back the river with his bare hands." We watched them get into their separate cars. "The worst thing for him is, he thinks he's doing it. You know what I mean? He's been swept out to sea already, but he still thinks his hands aren't even wet." She put her arms around my back, her cheek against my chest.

"Do you think he loves them?"

"He never loves them. He never even becomes their lovers. All those beautiful girls." She turned her face up to mine and looked into my eyes. "Come back inside with me."

Looking into her eyes confused me. I became in-tensely aware of her body nestling into mine. Her lower teeth glistened behind her full lip smiling, and her kiss was long and steady, her mouth full of the warmth of being wanted again. As she pressed herself more tightly against me, her whole long soft body hard against mine, I thought of our kiss in the shadow of Mt. Washington, the cold sunshine and the smell of evergreen, her sinuous body merging with mine for a moment, that impossible instant, the welcoming farewell. I wished things could have been different. But they weren't. I didn't belong there. Layer by layer the past increasingly separates us. Leslie and Alice and Sarah. She kissed me again, and I began to feel more lonely than I ever have in all my life.

CHAPTER **18**

Let the Lies Begin

Alice

Whispering cloth and crunching stone—Alice tried to separate the sounds. She lay with Jake on a yellowed futon in the front bedroom, under the open window facing the driveway. The walls and ceiling enclosing them were all sheathed with a cheap veneer meant to resemble gray weathered boards— sawdust and glue trying to call up salt air and wind-driven sand. She'd covered the paneling where she could with calendar pictures of flowers and gardens, French Impressionist prints cut from library books, her own photographs—of her son Christopher, her dogs and her kennel, the house she'd built with Matt. Her bedroom was broad and barren—a solitary meditation cushion red and yellow against the far wall, clothes still in cardboard boxes, a stereo alone on the floor in the corner. The mattress lay directly on thick green wall-to-wall carpeting.

As Jake pulled her shirt over her ears she thought she heard tires on gravel. "Wait," she said, as soon as her mouth was clear of the fabric.

"Alice," he murmured, kissing her. "You've been waiting for years." He slid his hands down her shoulders and began to unfasten her bra, fingers tracing her skin feeling exactly as she'd imagined they would, but again she heard *something* and she furrowed her brows, listening. She flicked her head with a habitual gesture of alertness—a slight jerk of her face toward her right shoulder, to toss long hair out of her eyes—rendered unnecessary, suddenly foolish, by her new permanent. The inside of her lip hurt where she unconsciously bit it.

The bra's fastening came free. The straps tickled her shoulders, then Jake's beard was lightly scratching her breast. Suddenly his lips and teeth were hard on her nipple; she felt a glow center between her legs, an aching she thought she'd never feel again. Still, she rolled away and sat up slightly, listening, listening: "Wait." She had a sudden unwanted image of Patti standing beside her on her wedding day, circlet of apple blossoms in shining black hair, dark eyes huge and naive as a doe's. "Jake, stop." His hands were pushing down her shorts and panties, his beard tickled her belly. She felt his tongue and lips between her legs. Patti's image shimmered at the edges, blurred, disappeared altogether. Alice's legs spread; she closed her eyes. A truck door slammed. "Jesus, Jake," she said, snapping her legs together so hard his head burst into her lap. "What if it's Patti?"

"It can't be Patti," he said. "It's way too early." He nuzzled back down and tried to force her legs apart with his mouth and chin. The screen door banged and the downstairs filled with children's voices, flooding the kitchen, the living room, swirling around the landing of the stairway itself.

Alice rolled away abruptly and quickly drew on her panties and shorts. She was fastening her brassiere when the voices stopped outside the door. Little knocks started and the doorknob began to turn. "Wait a minute, you guys," she called, looking for her shirt, trying to remember whether she had locked the door, but she could only recall the rush and power of Jake's kisses, too inevitable to really surprise.

Jake stood by the window, next to the cinder block and board bookcase he had set up for her when he helped her move. "Damn. It *is* Patti," he said. "What's she doing back so soon?"

Patti called from below, and Alice thought she heard all the children's voices disappear down the stairs. But when she opened the door Christopher was still there. And Brittany stood behind him, her thumb jammed into her mouth. Alice glanced back into the bedroom. Jake was pulling up his zipper. He turned away.

Patti called once more and Brittany went downstairs. Christopher stepped forward and wrapped his arms around Alice's knees, as high as he could reach. Alice bent down, kissed him and picked him up. Christopher hugged her neck and peered over her shoulder at Jake, his breath hot in her ear. She said, "C'mon," and carried him downstairs to the kitchen, where Patti was peeling a banana for Megan. There were two bags of groceries on the shelf. Brittany was peeling a banana for herself, squeezing the bottom hard with one hand and trying to break the short stem with the other. She put the stem in her mouth, bit it and made a face. When she pulled down one side of the thick yellow skin, the top half of the fruit broke free and fell on the carpet. Brittany squatted down, picked it up and began pulling off the bigger pieces of fuzz and lint.

"Hey, Brittany, that's dirty now," Alice said. Her smile flickered at Patti. "Thanks for doing the shopping. And taking Chris." Her son squirmed in her arms, reaching out for a banana. Alice put him down, peeled one, and gave him half. She offered the other half to Brittany, who shook her head, so she ate it herself.

"It's okay, we had a good time," Patti said, flashing her crooked grin. Alice's smile wavered; she turned away and busied herself unpacking groceries. "Besides, you deserve a break," Patti continued, tucking her long hair behind her ear. "I got your videos. I didn't make it to the hardware store, though—I must have lost Jake's list. Or else he never gave it to me." She looked around, large eyes questioning. "Where *is* Jake, anyhow?"

Alice hesitated, searching for words—it was hard enough just to meet Patti's eyes. She felt too splintered to answer, split and re-split, her separation from Matt still huge and raw, her separation from Patti just a matter of time now. The upstairs door banged closed. "Upstairs. I asked him to look at the bedroom door. It's sticking."

Jake came into the room. "Patti," he said, "Welcome back." He gave her a smile so big and false Alice was sure she would see through it. "I've decided to make some proper bookcases for Alice," he announced. "In return for letting me use the cellar for my shop."

Patti frowned, her hands on her hips. "*Another* project here." She looked from one to the other and shook her head. After a moment she said, "I thought the door was stuck."

Alice nodded, "It is." She continued to unpack the groceries. "You don't need to do that, Jake. The shelves I've got are just fine. Thanks, though." She put boxes of macaroni and cheese into the cabinet. "What *did* you decide about the door?"

"It's warped. That door is definitely warped." Jake took a beer from the half-empty bag. "I can take it off its hinges and plane it, though. Won't take more than an hour. I'll do it this afternoon." He twisted the top off and drank half the bottle. "Ah, righteous," he said, licking his lips. He wiped his mouth and beard with the back of his hand. His even white teeth glistened.

"Not *this* afternoon," said Patti. "I came back early so we could go to the lake. You too, Alice, and Christopher—if you guys want to come." Alice nodded noncommittally.

Megan approached Patti slowly with her ponderous walk. She pulled on the ragged fringe of Patti's cut-off jeans, her eyes like her mother's—dark and surprised. Patti glanced down, sniffed, said, "Uh-oh, Megan," and got a diaper from her bag.

Jake said, "I need to finish these cabinets for the Proutys. Did you get the hinges?"

Patti was squatting on the green rug next to Megan, unfastening her diaper. "You never gave me the list."

"Yes, I did. I left it on the front seat of the truck. Jesus, Patti, you mean you *didn't* get them. I told the Proutys I'd deliver the cabinets tomorrow morning."

"Tomorrow morning?" She slid the soiled diaper out and wiped Megan clean. "Are you planning to work here all day? It's Saturday, for Christ's sake." Patti smoothed down the strips of the new diaper, set Megan on her feet and patted her bottom. "There." She rolled up the old diaper and dropped it in the wastebasket. "We're taking the kids to the beach, Jake. We never do anything together anymore. It's like you live *here* now."

Jake walked over to Patti and hugged her. He ran his hands down to the small of her back and pulled her toward him. "It's a good job, Patti. We need the money, and I won't get the last payment until the job is finished."

Patti sniffed his neck and face. "You smell like *sex*," she said, her voice amazed and full of disbelief. She abruptly pulled back. She studied them both. "What's going on here?" She turned on Alice. "Jesus, Alice, you're..."

"Patti," Jake said, stepping quickly toward her again. "That's *you*, from this morning," he said quietly. "In my beard."

Patti hesitated and looked at Alice. "Then you should wash your beard, Jake."

Alice didn't hesitate. From a place she didn't know she had she looked right into Patti's face and said, "God." She shook her head slowly, but after a moment she had to turn away. "God, Patti." Tears blurred her vision and threatened to spill down her cheeks. She wasn't certain why she would cry, or for whom. She rubbed her forearm across her eyes, took a washcloth from the sink and busied herself cleaning Christopher's face. She wiped banana from Megan's mouth and cleaned Brittany's hands. Brittany was watching her father intently. "Brittany, take Megan and Christopher out to the sandbox," Alice said, controlling her voice. She rinsed out the washcloth and remained at the sink, washing her own hands slowly in the hot soapy water.

"I'm sorry," Patti said, after the children were gone.

Jake said, "Jesus, Patti, you *should* be. Alice needs your support now."

"I *said* I'm sorry," she replied, her voice trembling.

"You're so paranoid," he muttered. "Alice is your best friend." Patti stared at him, then she started to weep.

"Stop it, Jake," Alice said, hugging Patti, stroking her back with wet hands.

The children came back in, banging the screen door three times. "Mommy's crying again," said Brittany.

"Hurt?" said Megan.

Patti turned toward them, sniffing, smiling hard. "No. No, it's okay." She bent down to the level of their eyes. "How come you kids came back in?"

"Apple juice," said Christopher.

Alice opened the refrigerator, stocked full of milk and cheese from the WIC program, and took out a glass jar. She took their plastic cups from the dish drainer, noticing a slight tremor in her hands as she filled them and snapped on their lids. "Outside," she said. "Come on." She carried the cups to the door. "Brittany, can you open the door, please?"

She followed them out, aware of Jake and Patti talking, voices rising behind her. Megan and Christopher were dressed only in diapers, and from the back they looked like twins. Holding on to the plastic handles of their cups with both hands, they waddled away across the deck, toward the lawn and their sandbox. The summer air was intense with the fragrance of cut hay, and Alice breathed deeply a couple of times. She wiped the sweat from her temples. Lying was intense, too. It felt like playing with snakes, not daring to breathe, waiting for the bite. She wondered what Jake and Patti were saying.

And then the infiltration of anger began, anger spreading like venom, burning, throbbing into outrage. The thought of Jake and Patti making love that morning left her feeling betrayed. Lovers shouldn't overlap. They should be sequential, a linear continuum, with decent periods for mourning. Penetrating everything was that first limitless hurt of unfaithfulness.

It was indecent. After all these months of loneliness, loneliness for Patti's sake, her children's sake—refusing Jake, denying herself. Denying the *years*, actually—sexual attraction electric from the beginning, from their very first meeting, a lifetime ago, even before she married Matt. March night in Jake's sugarhouse, paradise, vapory lamplight. Steam and smoke and coalescing ghosts. Jake's tour of his world, his fingers vital, pulsing, his hand warm around hers, his arm strong at her back. Looking into his eyes and then just lost there. But these last months were impossible, unimaginably hard—these months since Christmas, since Matt interrupted them on the blue futon in the solar house. These months of Jake's relentless, incessant desire, and of Matt gradually going, of Matt finally gone.

Now every last thing was undone—all her sacrifice felt squandered, her friendship with Patti betrayed. She sat down suddenly on the edge of the deck, her feet on the broad step. She realized she couldn't trust Jake any more than Patti could. Probably less. Certainly less—Jake and Patti had been married four years. Once the lies began, trust vanished everywhere. What *were* Jake and Patti talking about right now? What if right now they'd gone to the core of this, found the deceit at the center, ripped it out? She would lose them both, Patti as a friend and Jake as...whatever he was to her. Things were changing so quickly. He still wasn't really her lover, not technically, not yet. But he wasn't just her friend anymore, either—that was all changing, changed. He certainly wasn't her man, her husband—although if that were to begin it could begin this way. Who knew anything?

She watched Brittany fussing with her cup at the edge of the sandbox. Brittany looked back at her, frowning. Alice considered her choices. Patti and Jake might still have the choice of returning to where they were, but she didn't. Once betrayed, Patti would never trust her again. And Jake? The only choice she'd had with him—between friends and lovers— she'd blurred years ago, given up to his hands, his strong hands, her body shining in his sauna house as he massaged oil into her skin, Patti and Matt lying stretched out on slatted benches above them, insensate with heat.

Brittany walked back toward her across the lawn, trying to pry the top off her cup. What were her choices now? Friendship, sexual love, loneliness? She knew some women whose friendships with men ended the moment they became lovers.

In any case—whatever happened—she'd already lost the deep dependability of her friendship with Patti. Alice concluded that she herself had already lost the most, and she remained the one who had the most at risk; she risked everything. She decided to go back inside. She stood up, then saw Brittany in front of her.

Brittany had outgrown cups with handles; she'd announced today she didn't need lids, either. When she reached Alice she handed the cup to her. It was greasy with banana flesh.

"Why is Mommy crying?"

"She's upset, Brittany."

"Is she hurt?"

"No. She's all right."

"Did Daddy hurt her?"

"No, Brittany." Alice smiled at her and took the lid off the cup. "She's all right. Don't worry. Here, sit down with me."

They sat together on the edge of the porch deck, swinging their feet. Sunlight warmed their bare legs. "Does Daddy live *here*, now?"

"No, Brittany, no." Alice put her arm around Brittany's shoulders and squeezed her. "Of course not. Why would you think that?"

Brittany scratched at a scab on her ankle. "I don't know. I'm scared sometimes."

Alice hugged her more tightly. "Poor little Brittany. Why?"

"Christopher lost his Daddy."

Alice stiffened. "Oh, no, Brittany. Christopher's Daddy isn't lost. He just has a new house now. Christopher sees him every weekend."

"You have a new house."

"We all have new houses now."

"*I* don't have a new house."

"Right. You still have your old house." Brittany drank some apple juice and seemed to consider this. She started to scratch her leg once more. "Don't scratch the scab off, Brittany. It will bleed again. When we go into the house I'll get you a new Band-Aid." Alice watched Christopher and Megan slowly pour their apple juice into the sand. "You have a nice house. Don't you like it?"

"Yes. I like my house. I like my room." She put her cup on the boards beside her. "Does Christopher miss his room?"

"He has a new room. He likes his new room very much."

Brittany was quiet for a minute. "Does Christopher miss his Daddy?"

"He has..." Alice stopped, not sure how to finish. She pulled Brittany up onto her lap and hugged her. "Sometimes he does, Brittany. We have to be extra nice to him."

Brittany climbed down from her lap, picked up her cup and walked across to the others. She sat at the edge of the sandbox, slightly apart from the two-year-olds. Alice watched her hold her cup out to Christopher. Megan reached for it, Brittany pushed her, and Megan started to cry.

Alice put her chin in her hands and closed her eyes. These children. Could she do that—just take their father? And Patti. Her best friend. Just take her man? Give Patti *her* place—suddenly a mother alone? That would make three fatherless children.

Megan stopped crying and the children began playing together in the sandbox quietly. Jake had finished that two weeks ago, the same weekend he fenced in the play yard with four-by-four pressure treated posts and chicken wire. It was a good job—his work usually was—and Alice admired it. The sandbox was an elaborate tiered construction with low benches all around and a place for a shallow wading pool.

Patti came outside. She had two beers and gave one to Alice. "Jake's not coming to the lake. He wants to borrow your car to get the hinges and finish those cabinets. Here, I bought some beer."

"Thanks. Sure, he can borrow it."

Patti sat on the hard decking of the porch and leaned against the house wall. Except for some toys, the porch was empty. Patti pushed a plastic truck with her toes. The children were having races between the sandbox and the fence. Brittany was giving the two-year-olds long head starts, then easily beating them. "Slow down, Brittany," Patti called, then turned to Alice and said, "I'm still after him to fence in a yard for Brittany and Megan."

"But you don't have any traffic there."

"Far from it." Patti held the beer bottle up. A heavy condensation had formed on the cold bottle and sunlight glinted off the beads of water. "So do you and Christopher want to come to the lake?"

"I don't know," Alice said. "I may just stay here."

"Look, Alice, I'm sorry about what I thought before. Things aren't great with Jake. You already know that. This morning was the first time we made love in almost a month. He's always too tired, or it's too late, or he's over here. I wish he hadn't set up his shop here."

Alice looked at Patti, then at the ground, then across at the children. She didn't answer.

Patti stared at her a moment, then asked, "How *are* you doing, Alice? Really?"

Alice looked across the lawn at the distant mountains, then she met Patti's eyes. "I'm all alone here."

Patti frowned. She crossed over to where Alice was sitting and put her arm around Alice's shoulder. "You're my best friend, Alice. God, we've been through so much together in three years." She shook her head slowly. "Pregnancy and childbirth...building our houses together. Your marriage."

"My divorce."

"You're just separated. You're not divorced yet."

"Five more months." Alice sipped her beer and thought for a moment. "It just gets so fucking hard. Christopher is always asking about Matt. Sometimes I wake up because Christopher's crying. I'll go to him and hold him and ask what's wrong and he'll say, 'I want Daddy.' I get so angry. He's crying and I hold him and he just says, 'Not you. Daddy.'"

Patti nodded. Alice flicked her head toward her shoulder. "I can't find a job, except for the little painting jobs I get from Jake once in a while. Matt never gives me enough money. And he never takes care of Christopher enough."

Patti squeezed her shoulder. "You'll make it all right. We could make it together. Start a painting and wallpapering business. Bring the kids on jobs with us—'Working Mothers, Inc.'" Alice laughed humorlessly. "I'm serious," Patti said. "We could probably get work at every single job Jake does, and branch out from there." Patti hesitated; she removed her arm from Alice's shoulder and ran her fingertip around the lip of the bottle. "It would be good for you. Help us both be more independent."

Alice sighed. "Thanks. That's a good idea. Jake's already offered to have me do all the staining and finishing of the pieces he builds here."

Patti turned toward Alice slightly; she put her hand on Alice's arm and looked into her eyes, then down at the wooden deck. "Look, Alice, this is really hard for me to say. I don't think it's so good for Jake to have his shop here." Alice stiffened and tried to draw her arm away but Patti held it and looked into her face. "Give us more space, Alice. Things are hard for us."

Alice nodded, swallowing. "But this a perfect place for his shop. There's no power at your place—how can you run a woodworking shop without power?"

"I know all that—Jake's explained that a dozen times."

"And it will be a lot easier to get materials delivered here, especially when the roads are bad."

"I know, I know that."

"And it's a big warm dry heated space for him to use in the winter."

"Jesus, Alice, *listen* to me," Patti said, squeezing her arm.

Alice jerked her arm free and jumped up. "Listen to *me*," she cried. "Nobody ever listens to *me*." She stalked halfway across the yard.

Patti was quiet, watching her. Finally she said, in the same low level voice she sometimes used with her children, "Don't be angry, Alice. I'm on your side. Come to the lake with us."

Alice hesitated, then shook her head. "Maybe tomorrow. Right now I need to be alone for a while. I think I'll go for a walk."

"Okay. Do you want me to take Christopher with us?"

"Thanks. That would be good."

Patti crossed the yard and hugged her briefly. "Things will get better. You can count on that."

"Things change—that's *all* you can count on," Alice said. It's when things start going well again that you really have to worry.

Alice returned to the porch after Patti and the children left. It was cold in the sunlight, and suddenly quiet. Sitting down on the rough deck, she wrapped her arms around her legs and pulled her knees to her chest. She wondered if love excused things, if it needed reasons or gave answers. She rocked slowly back and forth. She wondered if she and Jake really loved each other at all. Everything was all confused with lust and fear. She pressed her thighs together, tightened her

arms, hugged herself so hard she trembled. The world felt
scraped clean, a beggar's bowl empty of choices.

She thought about Jake and Patti. Jake was already
letting go. If it wasn't her, it would be someone else. They
were all just on cycles—coming out of pain before going into it
again. Patti was already on her own cycle. And Patti's pain?
Well—it had been her pain before, and one day, she knew, it
would be her pain again. Until thinking or feeling stopped,
anyhow. A kind of enlightenment at the end. At least freedom
from pain.

The screen door slammed the silence apart and Jake
came up beside her. He touched her shoulder gently. "Come
back inside." She nodded her head without smiling, and
followed him into the house. At the foot of the stairs Jake
embraced her. She hugged him for a moment, then drew back.
With two fingers he raised her chin, and brought her lips to his
mouth. She closed her eyes and shuddered involuntarily.
Everything changes. The lies begin. There are no reasons or
answers to anything.

CHAPTER 19

Blackberries

Matt

His hands looked perfect, pink, two-and-a-half years old: fat dimpled backs and pudgy fingers, nails as shiny as his stuffed bear's eyes. One hand still clutched his pacifier; the other was curled into a loose knot, his thumb in his mouth. Christopher held his bear in sleepy embrace, arm around neck, face against fur—the silver cub Matt had given him on their first weekend together in the new house. Two older bears lay at his feet. The parallel welts across his palm and fingers were hidden now, but Matt could see them anyway. He'd dreamed about them: red and raised where Christopher had grabbed the baking rack in the sink last night, glistening and still very hot, hissing up out of the soapy water. Matt winced as he heard his child's shriek again, felt the little tug where the flesh had stuck. In his dream, Alice had answered Christopher's shriek—torn him from Matt's arms to clutch him at her own breast, snarling at Matt like some savage beast as she backed away, all teeth and fangs, blood lust and maternal instinct.

Christopher had been trying to help him, standing on a chair in front of the sink and talking to himself, saying "oohhh, yes..." just before his unbroken scream began. Matt couldn't make him stop. Holding ice to his son's palm, he couldn't touch the terror or the pain. He walked around the kitchen with Christopher in his arms, stroking the back of his head, talking low words, trying to explain that hurt wasn't permanent, that time healed. But he was talking to himself, and to a child in diapers. His words were just soft lies in the roaring pain. Matt wanted to just *take* the child's pain away, take it onto himself with all the rest of it.

He hugged his son and rocked him, but Christopher wouldn't stop screaming. When Matt gave him the pacifier he spat it out on the floor—furious, betrayed. Matt went into the bathroom with Christopher howling on his shoulder, twisting and squirming in his arms. Cradling him against his chest, he unscrewed a child-proof bottle of Tylenol with his teeth. Christopher shoved the plastic bottle in his face, bawling, splattering them both with the bright red syrup. Shrieking in his ear and choking for air, Christopher thrashed, roared, louder and louder, until Matt suddenly screamed himself, clapped his hand over Christopher's mouth and ran with him to his room. He dumped him onto his low mattress and fled outside. Alone on the dark porch, Matt jammed his hands hard over his ears, but he didn't shut out the sound of screaming, and he couldn't stop trembling.

Now there was nothing but the sound of breathing. Christopher looked peaceful at the end of his nap—thumb and pacifier and bear—sleeping on his crib mattress on the floor in the old pantry. That was the first room Matt had fixed. He removed the filthy sagging shelves, spackled the holes in the water-stained walls, and reglazed the broken glass in the single window. He painted almost everything bright white—ceiling and walls, door and window casing. For the greasy wooden floor he chose a dark shiny blue. On the weekends he had Christopher, they made mobiles of bright colored paper— fantastic shapes that Christopher drew and Matt cut out. Together they glued them onto cardboard with sticky fingers and rubber cement, then strung them with fish line from coat hangers. Now they had eight—completely filling the white space over Christopher's head with outlandish swatches of primary color.

Christopher gripped his pacifier in his uninjured hand, fat fingers clenched around the rubber tip shaped like his mother's nipple, shaped to mold the plastic bones of his palate. Matt spoke his name softly; Christopher murmured and

stretched, then settled more deeply into sleep, smiling, so full
of grace Matt didn't want to disturb him again. He smiled
himself. For an instant everything made sense: love was all that
really mattered, and right now this small fragile person beside
him was the only thing that was keeping his ability to love from
being extinguished completely.

Matt let out a long sigh. He knew that in a few hours
he'd have to go through another exchange with Alice, trade his
son for that gutted feeling. He looked at his watch, then kissed
Christopher's forehead. He gently removed the Nuk, uncurling
each dirty finger. When Christopher shuddered and started to
cry again, Matt put the pacifier in his own mouth to moisten it,
then stuck it into Christopher's. He wondered if it was just at
his house that Christopher had so much trouble waking up, or if
he had the same problem at Alice's. He didn't remember the
problem from before, when they all used to share the same bed
together. They'd slept as peacefully as Buddhas then; Chris
would wake up smiling. Twice last night he'd woken crying.
And once, by accident, Matt had woken them both—calling out
Alice's name into the sweating darkness.

Matt walked the two older bears over the edge of the
mattress, calling one Chris, making them talk to each other,
appear and disappear under the red and white checked flannel
sheet. Christopher ignored the bears, sucking profoundly on
his Nuk; he looked hard at Matt for a long time before he
finally made a little smile. Matt picked him up and carried him
into the bathroom, hugging him tightly.

Half a century ago that room was the back parlor, in
the days before indoor plumbing. "Kitchen," Christopher said,
his Nuk dropping onto the floor.

"Your diaper, Chris. Time to change your smelly
pants." Matt set him down on the new bathroom rug and wet a
washcloth.

"Kitchen," he said, squirming, trying to reach the long
scarred table near the toilet. Matt had shortened the table's
legs, and painted it the same bright blue as the pantry floor.

Christopher's sink, stove, pots and pans were set up on the shiny dented surface.

Christopher grabbed a silver pot from the toy sink, spilling water over himself and the dirty cracked linoleum floor. With one finger Matt snagged the waistband of his diaper, pulled him back and laid him down on the rug, pinning him there gently with two fingertips on his chest. He stripped off the old diaper, grimacing, picked up Christopher's legs and quickly washed him. Matt dried him with a new towel, then used it to soak up the water on the floor before tossing it into the clawfoot bathtub with the stinking washcloth. He smoothed on a clean diaper, carried Christopher back into the pantry and set him on the mattress with his bears. Matt rummaged around in the drawers of the battered bureau, full of hand-me-downs from the woman at the general store. The bureau was another piece of furniture abandoned with the house—Matt had brought it down from an upstairs bedroom, painted the frame white and the drawer fronts bright blue.

"We're going on a Jeep hike, Chris," he said. "We'll need these pants," pulling out orange overalls. "And this shirt," he said, tugging the green and yellow striped jersey over Christopher's head. He tickled his fat belly. "And these shoes and socks." Christopher giggled. The sneakers were mismatched, part of a collection of salesman's samples the woman at the store had picked up at the dump. Matt finished dressing Christopher. "Hold still now. Double knots. Okay, come on."

They went into the big kitchen. Christopher started to whimper when he saw the sink; Matt shuddered and gave him another hug, then a rice cake with a cup of apple juice. Setting the day pack on the cold iron stove, Matt went around collecting a spare diaper, some insect repellent, a sweater for Christopher, his little hat, extra rice cakes, a canteen and the three bears.

Christopher sat in the middle of the floor, his eyes scanning the edge of the ceiling. The upper border of the kitchen walls were covered with a frieze of paintings he had made their first afternoon in the new place together, the grimy house empty and Matt with no idea what to do. He drove them to a store, bought some poster paints and brushes and two pads of white paper. They spent the afternoon splashing bright color in the dingy room. There were so many paintings Matt was able to staple them in an unbroken line around the kitchen's high perimeter.

They went out through the front parlor. A shortened table stood there, too, covered with picture books, coffee cans full of crayons and markers, and the poster paints, tops left off jars and the paint all dried and cracked. A pile of new sheetrock stood in the center of the room, bed-high and covered with Matt's sleeping bag and pillow. Alice had criticized him for sleeping on sheetrock: "You don't have to be a such a martyr. There are five old beds upstairs." She had lost touch with everything, though. That first night, he *had* slept on one of those upstairs beds, and all night long he dreamt of past sleepers there making love. He woke up convinced that something vital had been lost, bled out—that all the sadness left was hardening into permanent anger.

He felt Christopher tugging his pants leg. Matt picked up the orange jar of paint, spun it in the air with his thumb, caught it and handed it to him. Christopher carried it out onto the porch, then dropped it when he saw the cats. Squealing, he tried to catch one. Matt checked his pocket for the spare Nuk. Only one cat tolerated Christopher—Sunshine, the young neutered female. Matt picked up a couple of beer bottles and brought them inside. Alice would be picking up Christopher in just a few hours. Saying good bye to him at the end of each weekend was becoming the hardest thing for Matt to do, harder even than his confused feelings about seeing Alice. Losing Christopher over and over, these weekly encores of loss.

"What's that?" Christopher asked, pointing.

"That's your hoe, Chris. You know that."

"Shovel?"

"I don't know where you left your shovel. Maybe in
the barn. We'll check." Matt picked him up and carried him
down the short hill, his hoe banging against Matt's leg with
each step. In the barn there was a set of toy carpenter's tools, a
tiny bow with arrows, a pair of very short yellow skis, and
Christopher's miniature garden implements.

They found the shovel, and loaded it with the rake, hoe
and day pack into the space behind the Jeep's seats. Matt
shifted into low-range and drove across the brushy fields, past
the upper field barn, across the high pasture to the caved-in
deer camp just beyond the edge of the woods. They stopped
there where the logging road began, too grown over now even
for the Jeep.

Matt unbuckled Christopher from the car seat and
lifted him out onto the roadway. Christopher moved away,
unsteady and slow on the rough ground, legs stiff and gait
awkward. Matt stood watching him, thinking that, in some
ways, all the talk and argument notwithstanding—parents,
counselors, mediators, attorneys—no one ever paid any *real*
attention to Christopher. Adults defined the limits of a two-
and-a-half-year-old life, and then just worked on containment.

Christopher called something to him, but Matt had
stopped to consider the ruined deer camp. "Wait, Chris," he
said absent-mindedly. He pushed his finger into a damp,
greenish board. The roof had collapsed, and vines grew
through the walls. Some glass remained surprisingly unbroken,
glinting among soft, mossy wood. Someday the house he'd just
built and had to sell would look like that. It made his mouth
taste sour.

He didn't hear Christopher crying at first. He looked
up and saw him sitting on the ground, wailing, bright red blood
welling up out of a scratch on the palm of his burned hand,
shaking it as if he could shake away the pain. "Shit," Matt
said, hurrying forward.

Christopher held out his hand, looking scared and
confused. He was only a few yards away. Matt sat down,

pulled him onto his lap and hugged him. "Jesus, Chris, your poor hand." He washed his palm with water from the canteen, examined the shallow scratch, then hugged him some more. Christopher's crying slackened. "It will go away, Chris," he said. "The pain will go away." He smiled down at him. "Bye, bye, bad hurt."

"Bye, bye," said Christopher. He squirmed out of Matt's lap and stood in front of the briars that had scratched him, peering intently into their depths. Matt watched him, wondering how long it would take his own pain to go away. It felt beyond ever healing and made him feel like a liar to his own son. He extended his index finger. Christopher gripped it with his good hand and together they walked down the road. When they reached the next section of brambles Matt moved ahead and held the thorns out of the way. Christopher stopped. "Look, Papa," he said. "More berries."

"Um-hmm. Lots of berries. C'mon, Chris. Stay close behind me so you don't get scratched again." And good luck with that, he thought; I'm no guide for you. Thorns everywhere, lacerating wounds not even closed. The pain will go away, but the scar tissue won't. You'll lose some ability to feel, probably. It's a careless world we live in, Christopher, careless and uncaring. Matt looked back: Christopher hadn't moved. "Chris, hey, let's go."

"Papa. Berries."

"I know, Chris, I know. Lots of pretty berries. Come on, now." Matt stood in the path as Christopher came up to him.

"Berries, Papa."

"I see, Chris. Berries. Neat," Matt said. He looked at his watch. "C'mon, my little friend, time to go back. Your mama's coming to pick you up, and we need to be clean and ready for her." He squatted down. There was going to be hell to catch this time, when she saw his burned palm.

Christopher came right up to him. "Papa," he said, reaching out both hands and taking Matt's face, digging his tiny nails into Matt's cheeks like talons. "Papa, look." Matt grimaced, but didn't pull back. He could see himself caught in his son's eyes. "Listen to me," Christopher said, very slowly, linking the words together. "Berries, Papa. Berries you can eat." Then he let go of Matt's face, walked a step toward the brambles, and pointed to the blackberries among the thorns.

They lingered in the late afternoon sun for more than an hour, picking berries and eating them. Matt held each cane clear and Christopher plucked the juicy berries, studying the thorns carefully, smearing his mouth with the purple fruit.

Finally, gorged, with splotches like bloodstains all over his hands, Christopher brought blackberries to his father. He stood small and silent in the dusty roadway, clenching the fruit tightly in little fists. When Matt bent down to his level, Christopher reached out and touched his lips, then solemnly pushed the broken fruit into his mouth, one piece at a time.